Easton's CLAIM

The Colebrook Siblings

NEW YORK TIMES AND *USA TODAY* BESTSELLING AUTHOR

KAYLEA CROSS

Easton's Claim

* * * * *

Cover Art by
Sweet 'N Spicy Designs

* * * * *

ISBN: 978-1539011415

Dedication

For all my readers out there who love the friends-to-lovers trope as much as I do. It's one of my all-time favorites and I hope that after reading this story, it will be one of yours too.

Author's Note

Dear reader,

Here we are already, at the end of the **Colebrook Siblings Trilogy**. I've enjoyed getting to know this family, and I think I've saved the best for last.

For those of you who've asked, yes, Charlie will definitely be getting her own story. She'll star in one of the books in my new series, which will be about the DEA FAST squad guys. Woot!

Happy reading!
Kaylea Cross

Chapter ONE

"You seriously flew into town and then left again without even stopping by to see me?"

Easton Colebrook grinned at the outrage in his sister's voice. "It was only a pit stop, so I didn't have time, and that's why I'm calling you now. I'm already on the road."

"Why the big rush to get home? Dad's fine."

"No reason." A total lie. He was a man on a mission. In some ways, the most important mission of his life. But unlike all previous missions, conducted with his teammates to back him up, this time he was going in solo.

Charlie grunted. "I was thinking of maybe coming down for the weekend. Been a few weeks since I was home. I owe Dad a visit, and I guess it's the only way I'll get to spend time with you before you ship out again."

"Perfect, we can catch up then."

"You're up to something," she said in a suspicious

voice. "I can feel it."

Yep. "Nah. So what day do you think you'll drive down?" She worked for the DEA as a computer forensic examiner in D.C., just a few hours' drive from their family home in the Shenandoah Valley.

"Maybe Friday night, just depends on my work schedule. We've been doing a lot of overtime on this latest case."

"Can't wait to hear all about it. Look, I'm just outside of town now, so—"

"Okay, I'll let you go then. Say hi to Dad and Wyatt, and I'll see you on the weekend."

"Sounds good. Bye, Charles," he teased, because she hated it when he called her that.

He ended the call before she could respond and passed the sign that read *Welcome to Sugar Hollow* with a mix of peace and anticipation building inside him.

Four long months had passed since he'd last been home. Four months of dust and sand and grit, living in a warzone where enemy attacks could happen at any moment, and often did.

The constant grind of the deployment cycles to Afghanistan were starting to wear on him, and his body was beat up and sore. More than ever he craved the stability of home and family. Being here gave him the chance to recharge and unwind.

And to finally go after the woman he'd loved for more than a decade.

Piper had been on his mind constantly this last rotation. She'd been part of his life since he was thirteen, when she'd first moved to Sugar Hollow with her father as a high school senior.

Easton had still been too young for her to notice him back then, but even at thirteen he'd been pea green with envy that his eldest brother Wyatt had taken her to prom, then dated her briefly before leaving for boot camp at

Parris Island.

Easton had finished school and joined the Corps. He and Piper had remained good friends throughout those years but nothing more, and when he'd been discharged and come home, she'd been engaged.

He'd thought he'd lost her forever then, but over the past couple of years her marriage had crumbled. He hadn't realized how bad things had gotten. During his last visit home in May, he'd found out she was separated, and waiting to file for divorce. That day marked the first time he'd ever had a shot with her, and it had changed everything.

Including him. From that day on he'd severed contact with the handful of women he'd been seeing over the past year, his mind locked on one single goal: making Piper his.

Singing along to his favorite country song on the radio, he drove through the heart of downtown. Down Main Street, past all the brightly painted Victorian-style shops, restaurants and charming little B&Bs brimming with bright bursts of color from flowers spilling out of hanging baskets and window boxes.

No matter how much the world changed, the unique core of Sugar Hollow never did. He took comfort in that.

Two miles out of town he turned west, out toward the rolling farmland that made up the heart of the Shenandoah. It was late September, the days still warm and sunny, the nights crisp and cool. His favorite time of year. The oaks and sugar maples were just beginning to turn color. In another few weeks, the entire valley would be ablaze with spectacular fall color.

When he turned up the long driveway a few minutes later and his childhood home came into view at last, he let out a sigh of appreciation.

The two-story, pale yellow farmhouse sat in the middle of a sixty-acre parcel they used as a horse farm, handed down through the generations since before the Civil War ravaged the Valley. A lush green lawn spread out in front of it, and tidy flowerbeds hugged the base of the wraparound porch.

Coming home always relaxed him, reminded him of what was important in life. He'd have a quick visit with his dad, hit the shower, get a hot meal in his belly and turn in for the night. Tomorrow was a big day, years in the making, and he'd spent the past four months planning it carefully.

Everything hinged on how Piper reacted to what he was going to say, and he was nervous as hell about the outcome. Her douche of an ex had hurt her, destroyed her confidence. She'd always seen him as a friend, as Wyatt's little brother. So his feelings toward her were going to come as a hell of a shock.

It was a risk he was prepared to take, because now that he was home, he couldn't hold back another day. Whatever it took, he was going to show Piper that he was the man she was meant to spend the rest of her life with.

He parked out front of the house and grabbed his duffel from the back seat before climbing the steps up to the porch. As always, the front door was unlocked. Stepping inside, the familiar, comforting scents of wood, lemon soap and gun oil wrapped around him.

"Easton?"

Dropping his bag, he headed left into the study. His father sat at his desk, cleaning his favorite sidearm. Easton slid his hands into the pockets of his jeans as he stood in the doorway. "Hi, Dad."

His father's weathered face lit with a warm smile as he set his cleaning kit down, the right side of his mouth and eye drooping slightly. "Good to see you, son." He pushed to his feet and grabbed his cane to shuffle around the side of the desk, his plaid flannel shirt unbuttoned over an ancient olive drab USMC T-shirt.

Easton accepted the welcoming one-armed hug with a smile and wrapped his arms around his father's shoulders. They weren't as solid as they'd been before the stroke that had left him partially paralyzed, but they weren't frail, either. His old man was still tough as nails, and going to the local pool four times a week helped keep his muscles from atrophying.

Easton eased away but kept his hands on his father's shoulders. "You're looking good."

His gave a half shrug. "Can't complain."

He never did.

"When did you get back?"

"Yesterday afternoon." He'd gone straight to his apartment in Alexandria to shower and crash. After a solid twelve hours of sleep he'd done a load of laundry then packed up and headed here.

"Well it's a nice surprise. How long you here for?"

"About a week, maybe a few days longer, just depends." Provided nothing came up at work that he'd be called back for. "A buddy of mine might come out and spend a couple days here, not sure yet."

God knew the entire team could use the downtime this break afforded them, because this last rotation in Afghanistan had been tough. If he did, his friend would have to entertain himself for the most part though. Easton's priority on this visit home was Piper. Everything else was secondary.

"Jamie?"

Easton had mentioned their newest FAST team member to his dad in a couple of e-mails. "Yeah." The stroke hadn't affected his father's mind any. It was still as sharp as ever. "How are Wyatt and Austen? They set a date yet?"

"Nope, they want to finish renovating the house first, and I think they're waiting to see when Brody and

Trinity want to get married." Brody was the middle brother, and had just gotten engaged a few weeks ago.

"I still haven't met the mysterious Trinity, but she sounds interesting."

"You'll like her. She's badass."

Easton grinned at the description, because from his old man, those words were the highest form of praise. He just hoped he'd be stateside when his brothers got hitched, he'd hate to miss either wedding. "I'll go over and see Wyatt and Austen tomorrow." At some point he had to talk to Wyatt about Piper, and he'd have to tell his sister as well.

No one in his family had a clue how he really felt about Piper. And even after they'd broken up, Wyatt had always been insanely protective of Piper, so telling his big brother about his true feelings for her was going to be interesting.

"Charlie said she might pop down for the weekend as well, if she doesn't have to work."

"Yeah, I already talked to her." He was closest to her out of all his siblings, and the conversation about Piper needed to happen face-to-face.

Again, he was prepared for awkward. Charlie and Piper were good friends, and stayed in touch regularly. More than he and Piper had, with the exception of this last deployment, when he'd made a point of calling or e-mailing her at least twice a week.

He didn't think Charlie had noticed a change in his feelings for Piper, because she would have said something. There was no way Charlie would ever keep something like that from him; she would explode, trying to hold something like that inside.

"You gonna stay in here with me, or take the cabin? There's not much furniture in there now that Wyatt's moved most of his things to their house, but it'll still be comfortable enough," his dad said.

"Here's good." He didn't get much time with his family, so he wanted to make the most of this visit. "Maybe we can go for a ride tomorrow." It had been a while since he'd been on horseback and it always relaxed him.

"That sounds good," his father said with a fond grin. Now that Wyatt had moved out, it had to be lonely for him here. Even with his eldest brother coming by to help with the farm and take care of the horses with the other guys they'd hired on as part time help, it wasn't the same as having Wyatt live on site. "You eaten dinner yet?"

"No."

His father nodded and gestured for him to follow. "Come on, then. Let's see what I've got in the fridge that we can cook up."

Easton followed him out into the hall and into the kitchen, loving that things always stayed the same here at the farm. The bright, cozy room was spotless as always, the long farmhouse table dividing the open floor plan in half.

Over in the family room section, framed family pictures graced the white mantel. His mom had died when he was just a kid, and while he didn't have as many vivid memories of her as his brothers did, he could still see her presence in the house everywhere he looked. The comforting, familiar smells and sights of home surrounded him, but this homecoming was different.

His entire life was about to change, depending on what happened with Piper. It seemed like everything had been leading up to this moment, and now that he was standing on the cusp of it, raw exhilaration coursed through him, the biggest rush he'd ever experienced.

"Got some venison sausage in here. Want that with some eggs?" his dad called out, his head and shoulders hidden by the fridge door.

"Sounds good, but I'll do it."

"I can still cook," his dad said, pulling out of the fridge to aim a scowl at him. He hated it when anyone tried to coddle him. "How do you think I feed myself every day?"

Ignoring his father's grumbling protests, Easton made him sit down at the table, then took over in the kitchen. While he had the sausage cut up and frying in a pan, he beat the eggs in a bowl. "So," he asked, trying to sound casual. "You seen Piper lately?"

"Yeah, she was over last week. She likes to bring me a treat every now and then," he said with a smile, patting his belly.

The woman could bake like nobody's business. "And? She's doing well?"

"Well enough, I guess, all things considered. She's got her house up for sale."

"Oh." That surprised him, because she hadn't told him she was planning to sell. "Does she want to move closer to town or something?"

"No, back to Minnesota."

Easton whipped around to face his father as shock blasted through him. "*What*? When?"

His dad's graying eyebrows knitted together. "Whenever her place sells, I'd imagine."

Jesus Christ. This couldn't be happening. Not now. His pulse accelerated, his stomach knotting. "Why would she go back there?"

"Not sure, but she said something about a job offer, and I'm guessing to be with her father's people. Now that she's divorced and all alone, seems logical that she'd want family around her."

"*We're* her family." They had been from the time she'd moved here.

"Not the same as blood, I guess."

Bullshit. Her blood relatives could go fuck themselves for all the help they'd given her since her father died. Not one of them had reached out to her or come to visit since the day of the funeral five years ago. Not one of them cared enough about her to maintain contact. To Easton, his siblings and his father, she was family in every way that mattered.

Anxiety twisted inside him. They'd gotten closer through the e-mails and calls over the past four months, but they were still clearly in the friend zone. He hadn't wanted to tell her his true feelings any other way but face-to-face. Had he waited too long? Had he missed his shot with her?

He dumped the beaten eggs into the hot pan and quickly scrambled them, his mind spinning. God, what was he going to do? She couldn't move away, it would crush him. The instant the eggs were done he shut off both burners, scooped them and some sausage onto a plate and shoved it at his dad. "Here. I gotta go."

"Go where?" he asked, forehead puckered in confusion.

"To see Piper." And convince her not to leave. He couldn't let her go now, not when she was single and he finally had a chance to make her his.

Easton's heart raced as he headed for the front door. This couldn't wait until morning and he wasn't going to bother trying to talk to her about this over the phone. He jumped in his truck and tore down the driveway, headed for her house.

Chapter TWO

Piper tried and failed to ignore the way her traitorous heart skipped a beat when she pulled open the door and found Easton standing on her welcome mat. "Wow, hi! This is a pleasant surprise." The last e-mail from him four days ago had said he was still overseas and wasn't sure when he'd be back stateside.

He looked tired but good, his chocolate-brown hair cut short and a trimmed beard giving him a rugged, masculine appeal she'd have to be dead not to appreciate, even if she considered him to be like a little brother.

Or at least she had, until that day four months ago.

Ignoring that disturbing thought, she stepped back and let him into her entryway, foregoing the hug she normally would have offered because the idea of touching him that intimately made her jittery. "You just get into town?" Since joining the DEA's FAST squad a couple years ago, he only came home to Sugar Hollow a few times a year so she didn't get to see him much.

"About an hour ago." He didn't try to hug her either, which wasn't like him, just took off his boots and followed her into the kitchen. "Smells good in here. Whatcha making?"

"A batch of toffee chocolate chip cookies for the office. But I'll let you steal a few." She shot him a teasing grin and stopped on the other side of the swirled-marble island, where some cookies were cooling on a rack. "So, how are you?"

Damn, she was nervous. The kitchen felt three times as small as it had a minute ago.

Easton was the sort of man who walked into a room and took up all the space. He was just so…male, and sexy as all get out with that tall, sculpted body and those intense brown eyes. It was hell trying to pretend she didn't notice, but fighting it didn't work. Ever since the last time she'd seen him this past May, her brain refused to let her perceive him the way she used to.

"Good." He leaned a hip against the center island and set a roped, tatted forearm on top of it, his expression turning serious. "My dad says you're planning to leave town once your house sells."

Piper turned her back to him to hide her reaction. She'd never been good at masking her emotions and Easton knew her better than most people, so with him it was even harder. He could read her too easily and she didn't want to broadcast her mixed emotions. "Yeah."

"Why didn't you tell me?"

The bewilderment and hurt in his tone surprised her. Steeling herself, she turned back around to face him, squelched the jolt of yearning and attraction she didn't want to feel. "I wasn't sure until last week, and it wasn't something I wanted to tell you over the phone or in an e-mail." They'd been in contact more over the past four months than during the previous six years combined.

She'd eagerly anticipated each call and e-mail. Too much so.

"So you were just gonna sell your house, make arrangements to leave town, and call to tell me afterward?"

The frustration behind the words took her off guard. "I'm sorry, I didn't think you'd be so upset."

"You didn't think I'd be upset," he repeated, voice flat, eyes bleak when a moment ago they'd held such warmth.

She fidgeted with the kitchen towel in her hands, unsure what to say. "I didn't mean it like that." She knew he cared about her and would miss her when she left. Same as she would miss him.

"Then how did you mean it?"

"Well, I thought you'd be a little sad to see me go, but…" She trailed off, not knowing what else to say. She hadn't expected him to be this upset.

"And why go back to Minnesota?"

"They offered me my dream job, teaching humanities at a prestigious private school in a suburb of St. Paul, near where my uncles live." Where she'd been born and raised by her father after her mother divorced him and left for Mexico to be with her lover, leaving them both behind.

"Your uncles?"

"Yeah, I applied for the position months ago, and I wasn't sure I'd be qualified but they liked my credentials and charitable work. I flew out there for an interview a few weeks back, and just found out I got the job. I accepted, of course." She smiled, unable to hide her excitement. Teaching humanities had been a passion of hers for so long, and she'd given it up for Greg and his family. She'd been waiting for this chance, to reclaim her life and start over, and couldn't wait to be back in the classroom again. "Isn't that great?"

Easton shook his head, his mouth a flat line in the midst of his beard, a reminder that he'd just returned from another stint in Afghanistan. And that he'd be going back there again soon enough. She hated that his job was so dangerous. "You can't go."

They might be good friends, but that note of command in his voice made her spine go rigid. It was her life, and she'd fought damn hard to salvage it. No one was going to tell her what she could and couldn't do, not anymore. Not even him. "Well, I am. I thought you'd be happy for me." She'd be sad to leave Sugar Hollow and the Colebrook family behind, but she couldn't stay here anymore. It wasn't healthy.

"Why? We talked at least once a week while I was gone this last time, and you never once hinted you were thinking of moving away. So *why*?" He sounded so frustrated, she relented with a sigh.

"Because I need a fresh start." When he kept staring at her, she continued. "You've been gone for most of the last few years, but I'm sure even you heard people around town talking about Greg and me when you were here visiting."

He shrugged. "People always talk about shit that doesn't concern them. So I didn't pay attention to any of it."

Lucky you. "Well, I'm done with being at the center of gossip around here."

"Has it really been that bad?" he asked with a concerned frown.

Uh, *yeah*, but it was good to know her damage control efforts had mostly worked, if his cluelessness was any indication. Maybe not everyone in town thought she was a basket case.

She blew out a breath. It was embarrassing to have this conversation with him. He was a Colebrook, and as far as the people of Sugar Hollow were concerned, they were local heroes. At least Easton would never judge her. He'd known her for a damn long time, and no matter what, she knew he respected her.

"Greg pretty much ruined my reputation." *And my life.*

Looking back, she didn't know how she'd missed all the warning signs early on. The marriage hadn't been perfect, but in the beginning it had been pretty good. Greg had always liked to drink and have a good time. No one loved parties and attention as much as he did.

Then, to deal with the stress of his job as sheriff and what she suspected were issues he'd brought home with him from his deployments to Afghanistan years earlier, he'd started drinking more and more soon after their wedding. Not long after that, he'd begun abusing prescription meds and, eventually, harder drugs.

That's when his life had fallen apart completely, and whether he'd meant to or not, he'd dragged her down into the muck with him. He'd lied, manipulated her and other people, racked up massive amounts of debt she'd been clueless about at first. A few months after he'd become sheriff she'd heard whispers, rumors around town, and noticed people giving her pitying looks.

God, she'd hated that. The shame was still with her, like a permanent stain on her skin. It was partly her fault, for not seeing it soon enough. And for hanging on to the hope that Greg would pull himself out of the downward spiral and once again become the man she'd fallen in love with.

It hadn't happened. "Because we were married, as far as everyone around here was concerned, I was guilty by association. Even after we split, people were still judging me right and left. You know what this town's like. Gossip's a hot commodity, and I'm done with being the juicy topic around here."

Things had gotten so bad she'd become a damn

recluse for the first six months after she left Greg, too ashamed to show her face in town. While she loved the Colebrooks and hated to leave them behind, she was desperate to leave this place and have a fresh, clean slate for the next part of her life.

Easton straightened and folded his arms across his chest, dragging her attention to the muscular breadth of it.

For the millionth time, she mentally berated herself. *Stop perving. It's gross.*

"And moving away's the solution?"

She lifted an eyebrow. "Yes."

"What about standing your ground and saying to hell with what anyone else thinks of you?"

She fought the urge to roll her eyes. "It's gone so far past that, I can't even tell you. I'm sick and tired of people whispering about me behind my back, and fed up with being associated with Greg and his shitty decisions."

"What did he do? Other than take it out on you," he added, his jaw tightening.

Easton had seen firsthand how erratic Greg's behavior had become when he was here last. He had stepped between her and Greg to end an argument when Greg had shown up on her front porch one night, accusing her of leaving him for Wyatt, of all people. It defied explanation.

"I'm sure you heard plenty from everyone else."

"I want to hear it from you."

Fine. "A lot of different things. Like being drunk or high on the job. Borrowing money from people and not paying them back. Not showing up for work at all because he was passed out somewhere. A few times his own deputies had to go out and hunt for him when he disappeared for days at a time on a bender." When they found him they'd carried him through the front door of their home while she died a little more from mortification. "I want to be known and respected for who *I* am, and be judged for my own self-worth, not constantly having to prove myself to everyone just because of what my ex did."

"So you're going to run away."

She hated that tone, the disappointed one that said she was a coward.

You are a coward.

With effort she tamped down her irritation, sought a calm tone. "Look. I need to start over, and I can't do that here, or even within a hundred miles of here. Can't you understand that?"

"No. You're stronger than that."

Not anymore. Not after the humiliation Greg had put her through.

She turned away again, busied herself with cleaning up the mixing bowl and baking equipment she'd used to make the cookies. A taut silence built between them and she was acutely aware of him standing behind her, his stare making her skin heat up. "Maybe we should change the subject."

There was one more big reason for leaving she had no intention of mentioning, of course. Her growing and unsettling attraction toward the man standing across the island from her. A guilty secret she would take with her to Minnesota and hopefully bury there.

"This is your home," Easton said finally.

She didn't look back at him. "No, it's *your* home, and your family's been here for generations. I'm just a transplant."

He let out an impatient sigh. "Look at me."

Steeling herself, she did, and her heart squeezed at the sight of him. Such a brave, loyal and good man. The sort of man Greg had fooled her and everyone else into believing he was.

Easton's expression was resolute. "Sugar Hollow is as much your home as it is mine, but it's not going to feel like it if you're not here."

Guilt sliced at her. Hell, she felt guilty even *having* this conversation, because she wasn't being completely honest with him, since he was a small part of the reason she was leaving. "I'm sorry."

He stared at her in disbelief. "That's it? Your mind's already made up and there's nothing I can say to make you reconsider?"

"I've thought about this a lot over the past year, believe me." Ever since she'd left Greg. "It's the right decision."

He blew out a breath and ran a hand through his hair. "Wow."

She hadn't anticipated him reacting like this. It was nice to know he cared so much and was going to miss her, though. "I'm sorry," she said again.

He stared at her, and there was something in his eyes she couldn't define. Regret? "Yeah, me too."

God, her stomach was in knots. She didn't want to spend what was likely going to be one of her last visits with him arguing. She reached for a cookie and held it up as a peace offering. "Want one? Still warm from the oven."

"No thanks," he said, his gaze lingering on hers, and for some reason it felt like he was rejecting her rather than the cookie. A sharp pain lanced her chest at the thought.

Keeping her expression neutral to hide the hurt, she set the cookie back on the rack and wiped her hands on the kitchen towel, hating this entire conversation. In hindsight she wished she'd just told him about her plans when she'd first applied for the job.

"How long do you think it'll take to sell your place?" he asked after a minute.

She shrugged. “In this market, who knows. Could be a few weeks, could take a few months.”

“So, not long.”

“No, not long.” A wave of sadness hit her at the defeat in his tone. Couldn’t he see there was no other way?

As hard as the prospect of leaving everyone and everything familiar behind was, it was for the best. If she stayed she’d never move forward. Not the way she longed to, and this job was something she’d always dreamed of.

“I’ll hate like hell to lose you,” he said quietly.

His wording threw her. Lose her? She snorted in annoyance. “I’ll still stay in touch. It’s not like I’m gonna move away and then cut you guys out of my life, for crying out loud.”

“I wouldn’t let you anyway.”

“Well, don’t worry.” For her, this was about survival. And this new, unsettling attraction toward him was simply one more reason for her to go. He’d never change. His job was demanding and dangerous, requiring him to be gone a lot, for months at a time, and he lived for that adrenaline rush.

That wasn’t what she wanted. After the disaster with Greg she wanted stability, someone solid and committed to making and sharing a life with her. She wanted to know what real love felt like, and she wanted to have a family someday. She wasn’t going to find any of that here.

Exasperated, she sighed and shook her head. “I need to get my life together again.”

He scoffed. “Please, you’re the most together person I know.” He waved a hand to indicate the house. “Look at this place. Spotless. I bet I could eat off the floor if I felt like it. You’re the master of organization. You juggle everything going on in your life while rebuilding yourself after a shitty marriage, and you made starting a brand new career in real estate look easy. God, you even volunteer your time to teach yoga classes three days a week on top of everything else," he added, pointing to her yoga bag sitting on a bench by the back door.

Her laugh held an ironic edge, because it was all so sad. Couldn't he see how superficial all this was? "The house is staged, Easton. I made it look this way so I could sell it faster."

Oh yeah, she was a certified expert at making her life and surroundings look good. At projecting an image to the world that said she had her shit together, when in reality she was scrambling to pull herself out of the pit of debt and depression her ex had left her in. She'd had to master that in a hurry.

She tossed the kitchen towel aside. "And you know what else? I hate yoga. I only teach it because I have to do something to keep from climbing the walls at night when I'm here all alone, and because I like to stuff my face with my baking, so I have to do some form of exercise if I want to fit into my clothes."

His gaze slid over her from head to toe, making her go still inside. "Well whatever you're doing, it's working for you."

Heat bloomed throughout her body and she chastised herself. Easton had always teased her like this. *He doesn't mean anything by it, idiot.*

She cleared her throat and fought the warmth creeping into her cheeks. "Whatever." Scowling at him, she bit into a cookie, barely tasting it as she chewed. God, the man drove her crazy, though she'd be damned if she let him know it.

He uncrossed his arms and set his palms on the countertop, making all the muscles in his arms stand out. "Have dinner with me tonight."

She dragged her gaze to his face, belatedly realized

the cookie was poised partway to her mouth. "What?"

"You know, dinner? The thing people eat at the end of the day?"

Why would he want to take her to dinner? He'd never asked her to dinner in the almost twenty years she'd known him. Did he feel sorry for her or something because she'd just admitted to being lonely? If that was the case, she'd feel even crappier.

"I can't, I'm showing some clients a few properties," she said.

"What about tomorrow?"

She had a showing scheduled for her house tomorrow evening, so that could work. "Why do you want to go to dinner with me all of a sudden?"

One side of his mouth quirked up, as though she amused him. "So suspicious. To spend some one-on-one time with you."

Part of her wanted to refuse, but another part craved what he was offering. And she'd be leaving here soon enough anyway, so what could one dinner hurt? "Okay. But you're not going to be able to talk me into staying, so don't even try. I've already got everything planned out. As soon as my place sells, I'm moving to Minnesota."

"Okay," he said, but his expression clearly said *we'll see about that*. "I'll come pick you up at six."

"No, I'll meet you somewhere."

His mouth curved in a sexy grin. The sensual and highly experienced mouth she shouldn't be thinking about. "You embarrassed to be seen in town with me or something?"

"No, of course not," she said with a dismissive laugh. Not embarrassed. More like terrified he'd pick up on her increasing attraction toward him if she didn't limit their time together.

God, she hoped her house sold in the next few days.

Chapter THREE

It's just dinner with an old friend.

Piper kept repeating that to herself as she got ready, but it didn't quell the nervous flutters in the pit of her stomach. When she met Easton at the restaurant in a little while, she wanted to look her best.

Yesterday's unexpected visit had been awkward and strained. She wanted to leave things between them on a better note, and to present the image she wanted him to remember her by.

Polished Piper. Together, determined, and in control of her life. Pretty much the opposite of how she'd felt since her marriage had begun to unravel.

She smoothed moisturizer into her skin and slipped on the cobalt blue halter dress. The fit skimmed her curves, hinting at them rather than outlining them, and it had a pretty ruffled hem that hit just below her knees. The vivid color made her skin glow and set off the golden blond waves that she'd left loose to spill to the middle of her back.

A pair of strappy high heels waited where she'd set them at her closet door. She put them on, paused to check her reflection. Maybe she'd put on a few extra pounds over the last six months, but this dress did wonders for her figure and confidence. Even if this wasn't a date, at least Easton would see her at her best, and hopefully remember her that way.

As she thought it, a sudden pang of regret hit her that nothing would ever happen between them. She waved it off, told herself she was being ridiculous. Even if for some reason he became interested in her that way, hypothetically speaking, there were plenty of reasons why they couldn't get involved. Good reasons.

She was six years older than him, for starters, and her history with Wyatt, albeit brief and non-sexual, still made things…weird. And this line of thinking was completely inappropriate. God, it was damn near borderline incestuous to even think about it.

A knock sounded at her back door and her pulse skipped. Maybe Easton changed his mind about her meeting him at the restaurant and had come to pick her up instead.

She hurried down the hall and past the kitchen to the mudroom. She didn't see anyone out the window in the top of the back door. Frowning, she pulled it open, then gasped and took an instinctive step back when Greg suddenly appeared from around the corner.

Run.

Her heart cartwheeled in her chest. She darted a glance at her purse, sitting there on the bench next to the door. Her phone was in it. If she could grab it and run out the front door maybe—

Her ex barged in without asking, his face a terrifying mask of fear as he shut the back door and strode for the kitchen, forcing her to walk backward to avoid him.

He'd lost weight since she'd seen him last. His

cheeks looked almost hollow beneath the thick, sable-colored stubble and there were dark shadows beneath his eyes. Her stomach muscles clenched as that frantic, deep blue gaze locked with hers.

Piper shook off her initial shock and stood her ground. The sheer *nerve* of him, showing up and barging in here. "What the hell are you doing here?" she demanded, raising her chin. Last she'd heard he was in Tennessee, doing a stint in another super expensive rehab facility his parents had put him in. Apparently as with every other time, it hadn't worked.

"I had to see you." He swallowed. "I'm in trouble, Piper. Big trouble."

She didn't care, just let the anger burn through her, giving her strength that chased away the fear. "Get out of my house."

Greg lunged forward and grabbed her upper arms, the desperation in his hold cutting off anything else she might say. A bolt of alarm streaked through her at the stark fear on his face. His eyes were clear, the pupils normal, and he didn't smell of booze. That was even scarier.

"Please, I need your help," he rasped, his expression earnest, his grip frantic.

He's clean.

The terrifying knowledge kept reverberating through her brain, made cold spread through her gut.

He wasn't drunk or high, hadn't shown up here driven by paranoia or some drug-induced hallucination. As former sheriff he knew better than anyone the repercussions of violating the terms of the restraining order. Whatever was going on with him, for him to show up here and risk going to jail meant the situation he faced was worse.

She had a sickening feeling he'd finally hit rock bottom and that his life was in danger. He must have finally pissed off or crossed the wrong person. A drug dealer. A drug trafficker. Maybe a gang, who knew.

Pushing aside the dread and anxiety, she found her voice. “I can’t help you. Now get the hell out before—”

“Your grandmother’s furniture.” His voice was ragged, the bite of his fingers around her upper arms bordering on painful. “It wasn’t in the storage locker. Where is it?”

He’d broken into her storage locker to look for it? What did he even want with it? God, he had to have done something really bad this time. Either that, or he was in so much trouble that he hoped being arrested would save him. She’d inherited at least a half dozen pieces from her grandmother, all stored in various places. Which piece was he even talking about?

“What the hell have you gotten yourself into?” she whispered, yanking free of his hold and taking a step back. Her skin crawled, the back of her neck prickling.

“I can’t…tell you.” Greg’s eyes were bleak, sad, and damn him, despite everything he’d put her through, it tugged at her heartstrings.

She might not love him, she might not even like him anymore, but she’d been married to this man and still cared about him as a human being. He hadn’t always been a junkie. It saddened her that his life had turned out this way, even though it was his own doing. And right now she had a bad feeling someone was out to kill him. There was no other explanation as to why he would do this.

Whatever his faults, she didn’t want him to die. She had to call the cops. “Out of my way, Greg,” she commanded in a voice that sounded much braver than she felt. She took a step around him but he blocked her with his body, the perspiration on his forehead standing out beneath the kitchen lights.

“Tell me where it is, Piper. If you ever cared about

me, tell me now."

A shiver rippled over her skin. She fisted her hands at her side and edged away from him, toward the mudroom. Was someone targeting him at this very moment? Were they coming here?

She'd grab her purse, run, then call the cops once she was safe. "Only the pie chest is here. Everything else is in storage."

"There's a dresser," he insisted, his eyes wild. "It wasn't in the storage place."

Because some of the pieces were in a shed at the Colebrook place. "Then I don't know."

"God dammit, you have to know!"

"What did you do?" she demanded, her voice shaking.

She didn't tell him where all the furniture was, because she wanted no part of whatever trouble he was in, and just wanted to get the hell out of there. This had to be drug or debt related, and he was scared shitless.

Her chest tightened. Had he just put her at risk by walking in here, into her home? Were the people after him now going to come after her, because they linked her to him again?

"It's better if you don't know. Just tell me where it is."

The cryptic words were the last straw. Piper whirled and rushed for the back door. Her heart slammed against her ribs at the sound of thudding footsteps behind her.

Just as her hand shot out to grasp the knob, Greg grabbed her shoulder and yanked her back toward him. "*Piper*." His sharp voice cut through the tension like a whip. "I need it, do you understand? They'll kill me otherwise. Tell me where it is."

"I told you, I don't *know*." She clawed at his hand, ready to fight him tooth and nail to get free if she had to.

He was bigger, far stronger, and he was trained, both

by the military and then law enforcement. She was counting on him having one last shred of decency to release her before things got ugly. Even during their worst fights when he'd been wasted, he'd never physically harmed her. But he'd never been afraid for his life before, and she didn't know what he was capable of now.

"Think, dammit! You must know where it is!"

"Let me *go*," she said between gritted teeth, then wrenched her arm free.

Her legs shook as she snatched her purse from the bench and darted out the back door, heading for her car parked in the driveway.

Behind her Greg was shouting her name, the terror and grief in his voice sending chills down her spine but all she could think about was getting the hell away from him. She caught a glimpse of him standing on the side doorstep as she backed onto the street. She didn't pause, just threw the car into drive and hit the gas.

Shit, her hands were shaking. Paranoia and lingering fear kept her checking her mirrors as she sped down the street, but she didn't see anyone following her. At a stop sign a few blocks away she fished out her cell phone and dialed 911.

Her throat was tight, her entire body trembling as she relayed to the operator what had happened, and that Greg had violated the restraining order. The operator told her to stay calm and assured her the police were on the way to her house.

Piper ended the call and set the phone down in her lap, afraid to stop driving. Greg was screwed up, but he wasn't stupid. He'd be long gone before the cops arrived to pick him up. But what about her? What if whoever was after him had seen her? They might come after her now. And her car was red, easy to spot.

Easton. She had to tell him. He'd know what to do.

She dialed his number, gripping the steering wheel tight with her free hand as she drove through town and prayed that he'd pick up.

****

Easton's phone rang while he was in the middle of getting dressed. *Piper.* He smiled as he answered. "Hey, beautiful. What's up?"

"Greg just barged into my house, demanding to know where my grandmother's furniture is. And he was *clean*."

The distress in her voice slammed into him like a punch to the gut. He froze in the act of shrugging into his button-down shirt. "What? Where are you?" He whirled for the dresser, grabbed his keys.

"In the car."

He started for the door, not bothering to finish buttoning his shirt. What the hell was going on? "Are you safe?"

"I think so. I got out as soon as I could and called the cops. They're on their way to my place. If he's still there when they arrive, they'll arrest him. He thinks someone is after him, and from the way he was acting, they have to be close."

If he was clean like Piper had said, Greg would be long gone before the cops got there. Shit. "Where are you now?" He kept his voice calm as he rushed down the stairs, quickly shoved his feet into his boots.

"I'm just outside of town. I didn't know where to go."

She sounded so lost, it sliced at his insides. His father got up and shuffled out of the den but Easton shook his head and rushed out the door. "You wanna come here?"

"I don't know if I should. What if someone was following him, and now they're following me?"

Ah, hell. "Go somewhere public and wait for me there. I'll meet you. I'm leaving now." He just wanted to get to her, make sure she really was okay. And if Greg or some other asshole had followed her, Easton would take care of it.

"Okay." She named a gas station just off the highway.

"I'll be there in fifteen minutes. Don't move from there, okay?"

"All right." She let out a shaky sigh. "I'm sorry about this."

"Nothing to be sorry for." *Damn you, Greg.* "Just hang tight. I'm getting into my truck." The door alarm chimed as he climbed into the cab. "Want to stay on the line with me until I get there?"

"No, it's okay. Think I'll just park and get myself together before you get here."

"No need, sweetness." He didn't want her to have to compose herself before seeing him. He wanted her to feel comfortable with him no matter what was happening. "Call me if you want in the meantime, okay?"

"I will." A pause. "Thanks, Easton."

"No worries." He was halfway down his long driveway when he ended the call. By the time he'd reached the gas station, he was livid. He couldn't believe that lowlife asshole would drag Piper into whatever shit he'd gotten himself into this time. Wasn't Greg supposed to be in another rehab program out of state right now?

He spotted her little red car next to the service station building and pulled into the parking lot. She climbed out of her car as he parked beside her, her expression sheepish.

And mother of Christ, she looked sexy as hell in that deep blue dress, her golden blond hair all shiny and spilling down her back in soft waves.

"Hey. Thanks for coming," she said as he got out of his truck.

He didn't want her thanking him for that. "You all right?" he asked, placing both hands on her shoulders, her skin warm and smooth under his palms.

She nodded, staring at the middle of his chest where his shirt gaped open. He wished it was because she wanted to look at his naked chest, and not because she was embarrassed. "I'm fine. This was just…a shock."

Easton settled his hands on her back and drew her into a gentle hug instead of crushing her to him the way he wanted to. His girl was shaken and afraid and he'd do anything he could to protect her and make it better.

His heart beat faster when her arms encircled his waist and she leaned her cheek on his shoulder. Her soft floral scent teased him, her warm curves nestled against the hard planes of his torso. She felt amazing and he had to force himself to drop his arms and release her before she noticed the erection growing in his jeans. "The cops call back yet?"

"No. I'm sure he would've left when I did. Maybe they're out searching for him."

Maybe. "Can I do anything?" God he hated seeing her sad and worried.

She shook her head, lowered her gaze to the pavement between them. "This is more than enough."

Not by a long shot, but his plan for the evening was all shot to shit now, so his campaign to woo her was going to have to wait. "Come into my truck and tell me what happened."

When she climbed in, he noticed the thin gold chain wrapped around her ankle. "You still have the anklet?"

She glanced down. "Yeah. I always wear it. It reminds me of you. You gave it to me for my birthday one year, remember?"

"Of course I remember." He'd been fifteen when he'd given it to her. His dad had pitched in the extra thirty bucks Easton hadn't been able to come up with in time for her twenty-first birthday. If his old man had guessed at his true feelings for Piper back then, he hadn't said anything. It touched him to know it still meant so much to her. "I'll have Wyatt and Austen come pick up your car and drive it to the farm."

"Okay."

Rather than sit in the parking lot, he drove them back toward town while she filled him in on what happened. He kept checking his mirrors to make sure no one was following them, just in case. "What would he want with your grandmother's furniture, anyway?" They'd split almost a year ago now. She'd been waiting for the anniversary to hit so she could file the divorce papers, and that had been two months ago. Why would Greg suddenly want anything of hers now?

"He must have hidden something in it. It's the only thing I can think of."

Weapons? Drugs? Money? Anything was possible when it came to Greg. The once proud and celebrated Army vet had sunk to new lows before Piper had left him. It infuriated Easton to think of her being subjected to that kind of treatment, being humiliated and ruined by the man who'd vowed to protect, honor and cherish her for the rest of his life.

Easton had heard the vows firsthand, because he'd been at their damned wedding. He'd gone for her sake, and her sake alone, dying inside as he'd watched her pledge herself to another man.

That's all he remembered, because as soon as the ceremony ended he'd left and gotten shit-faced drunk to avoid thinking about losing the woman he loved. Easton had known even then that Greg had a drinking problem, but even he wouldn't have guessed how fast things had gone downhill after the wedding, or how bad it had been for Piper.

Whatever shit was going down now, Easton would be damned if he stood by and allowed Greg to hurt her anymore.

"You still hungry?" she asked, taking him by surprise. "I was in the middle of getting ready to meet you when he showed up."

He'd made reservations at a fancy B&B in the next town over, had intended to tell her that his feelings for her went way beyond friendship, but obviously now wasn't the best time to take her there and lay his heart on a platter. "I already canceled our reservations. Are you hungry?"

She made a face. "Not really, but I guess I should eat something. I was so busy today I haven't had anything since breakfast."

"What do you feel like?"

"I don't care." She'd put on a confident façade over the past few minutes, even though he knew perfectly well she was still upset. It bothered him, because he didn't want her to feel like she had to pretend in front of him.

"How about we grab something quick? Feel like a milkshake?" She'd always loved the chocolate shakes from the diner just off the highway.

"That sounds perfect," she said with a relieved smile.

He drove them there and grabbed milkshakes and fries to go. When he came out she was on the phone. Her hazel-green eyes met his from across the cab of the truck, wide and full of shock. Easton shut the door behind him, set the food down and waited, his muscles tensing. What now?

"Yes, okay, I'll be there as soon as I can." She ended the call and looked at him with haunted eyes, her face so pale the smattering of freckles on the bridge of her nose stood out. “Greg wasn’t there but the police said my place was trashed. There was apparently some kind of struggle and there are bloodstains…” She hitched in a breath. “I need to get to my place as soon as possible.”

Chapter FOUR

When Easton pulled up to the curb in front of her house a few minutes later, Piper's stomach was a giant knot of anxiety. The driveway was blocked off with police tape and patrol cars lined the street on both sides. Neighbors were out watching from their lawns and staring from their windows, waiting to see what was going on. That old familiar shame crawled up her spine.

Oh God, I just can't deal with this shit anymore.

Dreading what she would find inside, she got out of the truck and started up the driveway, Easton right behind her. They hadn't spoken a word on the drive here. As much as it humiliated her to have him see yet another example of the kind of shit she'd dealt with in the last few years of her marriage, this was by far the worst and she was glad to have his steady, solid presence there to bolster her.

A group of deputies were standing on her front porch. She knew pretty much every deputy in the area, and thankfully they had all been friendly with her after she'd left Greg. One of them detached from the others and started toward her. When he stepped out of the shadows and into the sunlight she recognized Frank, a thirty-something deputy who used to work with Greg.

"Piper. You all right?"

She forced a nod, her heart thudding against her sternum. "How bad is it?"

"There's a fair amount of damage."

Ugh. "Can I go in?"

"Not yet, the forensics teams are still working inside. And Greg was definitely attacked and kidnapped. One of your neighbors saw him being dragged out of the house by two men."

"Oh, Jesus," she whispered, feeling sick at the thought.

His gaze shifted between her and Easton. "Come sit in my patrol car and tell me what happened," he said to her.

She glanced at Easton, who nodded, then followed Frank to his car. After rehashing everything that happened with Greg, he told her what they'd found so far, then radioed the forensics team and got the okay to bring her inside.

Before letting her out, he paused, his eyes full of sympathy. "I'm so sorry about all this," he said. "I hate seeing him wind up like this."

Yeah, her too. "Any leads yet?" Whoever had come after Greg must have shown up within minutes of her leaving, because the cops had arrived under ten minutes after her call.

Her neighbor had seen two men put Greg, who had appeared unconscious, into a black car and drive off. Whoever had taken Greg might have seen her, waited for her to drive off before attacking. It made her skin crawl to think that someone that violent had been watching her and her house.

"No. We'll need to get the samples analyzed before we know if it's his blood or not. It's not a large amount, so whoever was injured, we don't think it's severe. And if the attackers wanted to kill him, they would have just done it and left him here. So there must be some reason he was taken alive." He straightened and reached for his door handle. "You ready?"

"Yes." Bracing herself, she climbed out onto the foot of her driveway. Easton pushed away from his truck and started toward her.

"Want me to come inside with you?" he asked.

"Yes please," she murmured, thankful he was here.

He stayed close beside her as they followed Frank up to the front porch, but didn't touch her. Officers and techs moved out of their way as they approached, and Piper hated the pity in their eyes.

It was happening all over again. By morning the entire town would be abuzz with rumors and gossip, and her good name would once again be tied to Greg and this incident as people speculated about what had happened. Yet another reason she wanted to get the hell away from here, but this latest incident meant her departure was going to be delayed even longer.

Even though she'd prepared herself for what she was about to see, she still sucked in a breath at the first sight of her living room. Everything she'd staged so carefully to sell her home had been destroyed.

Tables, lamps and her desk had been overturned. The flat-screen TV was lying facedown on the floor, apparently ripped off the wall, bits of its plastic frame lying around it.

Books and other items she'd placed on the shelves of the built-ins on either side of the TV littered the area rug. Chunks of drywall were missing from the walls where something heavy had crashed into them. The framed prints she'd hung around the room were all lying smashed on the floor. Broken glass glittered in the sunlight streaming through the front windows.

Holy shit. Greg had put up one hell of a fight. It turned her stomach to think of him in here, fighting off two men. Maybe fighting for his life.

Easton set a hand on the small of her back, his touch comforting and warm, helping to melt some of the ice inside her. Her heart sank when she glanced toward the kitchen and saw her grandmother's antique pie chest toppled on the floor with a wide crack down the middle of its back and both doors broken off.

Sadness crashed over her. Of everything she'd lost today, seeing that treasured piece lying broken hurt the most.

"You said he asked you about your grandmother's furniture," Frank said beside her. "He or whoever attacked him had to be looking for something inside it. We searched all the older-looking pieces of furniture in here but couldn't find anything. Do you know if Greg hid anything in that one?" He gestured to the broken pie chest.

She shook her head. "I pulled this out of storage last week so I could stage the house. I didn't notice anything when I cleaned it." And now it was ruined. "Like I told you, the rest of the pieces are stored in the storage locker I rented, and I put some things in a shed at Easton's dad's place as well."

"I've made a note of all that for the file. If you think of anything else, let me know." He continued through the family room, heading toward the kitchen.

Piper stayed rooted to the spot, staring at the pie chest. It was much more than a piece of furniture to her. "It's from the 1870s," she said to Easton. Probably not worth much, but in terms of sentimental value, it was irreplaceable. "Whenever I stayed at my grandmother's house during the summers when I was young, she and I would bake pies and store them in there. She's the one who made me fall in love with baking."

Her throat tightened and tears rushed to her eyes. She blinked them back, bit her lip until she forced the wave of emotion back. Crying wasn't going to fix anything, and she was tired of everyone seeing her as weak. She didn't want Easton to think of her that way.

He rubbed her lower back gently, and she fought the urge to turn into him and wrap her arms around his waist. "I bet Austen could fix it. Wyatt and my dad say she's a carpentry wizard. As soon as we get your place back, I'll load it up in my truck and take it over to them."

She didn't think it was salvageable and was too overwhelmed by everything to respond, so she nodded her thanks and followed Frank toward the kitchen.

When she reached the threshold separating the two rooms her feet stuck to the floor at the sight of the bloodstains smeared all over the polished hardwood. A bloody chef's knife from the butcher block next to the sink lay on the floor, blood pooled around it in a glistening puddle. Crimson spatters were splashed onto the counter and up her cream-painted cabinets.

Her stomach pitched and she put a hand to her mouth. Was it Greg's blood?

Without a word Easton wrapped an arm around her waist and pulled her into his side. She stared at the knife she'd used to prep her meals, envisioned it being used against Greg. She swallowed.

"Want to step outside for a bit?" Easton murmured.

She shook her head, trying to take in all the damage. How had this happened? Greg was missing, possibly wounded or worse. Her house was a mess, a good number of her most precious things destroyed.

There was no way she could show the house until all

the repairs were made. Who knew how long the police would treat it as a crime scene? Then there'd be cleanup and repairs. She'd have to clear out all the broken glass and furniture, patch and paint the walls, replace all the furniture and deep clean everything before she could show it again.

"Everything else seems pretty much intact, but the forensics team is doing a thorough sweep of the entire house, just to be sure," Frank said.

Piper turned and followed him down the hall to the guest bath and bedroom, then into her master bedroom. The drawers of her dresser had all been dumped out, but from what she could see there was no damage here like in the main living areas of the house.

Staring at the contents of her drawers strewn over her floor and bed, her underwear, clothes and jewelry, she felt…violated. The thought of coming back here to tackle the clean up after the police turned the house back over to her filled her with despair.

After she packed a bag with clothes and toiletries, Frank walked them back outside and down the driveway. Piper was acutely aware of all the stares from neighbors and other curious onlookers walking their dogs past her house. At least one of them had witnessed Greg being dragged into the kidnappers' car.

The frantic need to leave built inside her, pressing at her ribs until it felt like her chest might explode.

As they neared Easton's truck, Frank stopped. "Do you have somewhere to stay tonight?" he asked her.

"She can stay with us," Easton said before she could answer. "My brother's driving her car there right now."

Piper met his eyes and forced a small smile. "Thanks." She wasn't looking forward to coming back here to clean up, let alone stay here by herself. At least at the Colebrooks' she'd feel safe and have a short reprieve before having to face reality again.

"It's a good idea to be vigilant over the next few days, at least until we find out what happened and locate Greg," Frank said.

"We'll look out for her," Easton said, drawing her into his side with a firm hand on her waist.

She didn't want to be a burden. She'd tried so damn hard to rebuild her life and regain her independence. This ugly incident threatened to undo all of it.

"Come on, sweetness," Easton murmured, and opened the passenger door for her.

They didn't talk on the drive to his father's place. When he pulled up out front and shut off the engine, she reached out to put her hand on his. "Are you sure it's safe for me to be here? I don't want to bring you guys any more trouble." They'd had more than their share of that lately.

"I'm sure. Don't you worry about us. How about for a change, you let us worry about you?"

She blew out a breath. "I hate this."

"I know you do. But at least if you're here, we can make sure you're safe."

"Okay. Thanks."

In the house he put her bag in Charlie's old room and when they came back downstairs, his father was waiting for her at the foot of them. He stood there with his left hand on the top of his cane, an unmistakable aura of power and authority radiating from him in spite of his deteriorated physical condition. His hazel eyes were full of empathy as he looked up at her.

She paused, hand on the railing, precariously close to tears. This man had become a father figure to her after her own dad had died. He'd never liked Greg. None of them had. She'd been naïve, had truly thought she and Greg loved each other enough to make it work. How wrong she'd been.

None of the Colebrooks had ever said *I told you so*

when she'd finally realized Greg was beyond help and made the decision to leave him, but it crushed her to think that she might have disappointed this strong, proud man standing before her.

"Hey, Mr. C," she whispered in a rough voice. "Sorry about dragging you into this, but thanks for letting me stay for the night."

That penetrating stare bored into her as he started up the steps, his cane landing with a thud on each tread.

He stopped on the step below her, bringing him eye to eye with her, and set a finger beneath her chin to force her to meet his gaze. "Young lady, there's nothing to be embarrassed about," he said, his words firm despite the slight slur in his speech. "Hear me? You're one of us, always have been, and we look out for our own. You're welcome here anytime, for as long as you like, no questions asked. Ever."

His kindness was her undoing. Tears flooded her eyes and her throat closed up. "Thank you," she choked out, and whirled past Easton to flee upstairs to Charlie's room where she could cry in private.

She loved these people with all her heart and leaving them behind would rip her heart out, but the nightmare that was her personal life wouldn't end until she got her house sold and left for Minnesota.

****

Not so arrogant now, are you, asshole?

Brandon pushed away from the wall where he'd been watching one of his men beat Greg Rutland to a bloody pulp and signaled for him to stop.

He stepped into the light so the prisoner could see him. Greg groaned and raised his head, struggled to open his swollen eyes, his hands bound to the chair he sat on. Blood spilled down his lips and chin and his breathing was choppy.

"From the way you hightailed it back here, I guess you heard the news that I was out," Brandon said softly, folding his arms as he stood in front of his hostage. He'd lost years of his life in jail because of this piece of shit. Time for payback. "Too bad you weren't quick enough to get what you needed and then skip town."

Greg dragged in a painful breath and leaned forward to spit out a mouthful of blood.

Brandon smiled at the sight. *Oh, how the mighty have fallen.* It filled him with a sense of vengeance to see his old enemy this way. Helpless and afraid. Wondering what would happen to him, unsure how far Brandon would go. But as sheriff Greg had been the one to put him behind bars, and had the unique privilege of knowing exactly what Brandon did to people who dared cross him.

Four years in federal prison. Four years of living with a depraved cellmate, of having every freedom stripped away. Of having to strip naked and have his ass searched. While the motherfucker in front of him had been free to live off his parents' wealth and do whatever he wanted—which turned out to be fucking up his life royally.

Brandon loathed Greg and his kind. A rich, trust-fund baby born with a silver spoon in his mouth. Parents respected professionals connected to society's elite. They'd bought him a new car when Greg had gotten his license at age sixteen. They'd paid for his college education and a swanky apartment off campus. They'd done everything but wipe his fucking ass for him. And how did their son repay them?

By snorting all the money they gave him up his nose and becoming the worst embarrassment Sugar Hollow had ever seen.

It disgusted Brandon. He'd been born poor and had

stayed poor until he started running drugs at the age of twelve, after escaping one abusive foster home too many.

That kind of poverty left its mark. He still smelled the stink of it when he woke up every morning. He still remembered the grinding pain of hunger when he went to bed at night. Even when his stomach was full, that grinding sensation was always in the back of his mind. He'd vowed at age fourteen to make sure he never lived like that again. For fifteen years, he'd had a good life. Financial security.

Until this fucked-up loser had taken everything from him with the arrest.

Brandon pulled in a deep breath and released it slowly, letting the anger drain away. Anger clouded his judgment. For this he needed to be calm, in control. Greg had betrayed him, used him to get product and then turned on him to save his own skin. He would pay. "I want what's mine. What you took from me."

Those swollen, bruised eyes focused on him. "I don't have it," he slurred out of busted lips.

"But you know where it is."

He shook his head slowly, winced. "No."

"Bullshit." Brandon was going to establish himself back into DC's drug scene. He'd lost face, respect of the people who'd once feared and admired him. He was going to make a name for himself again, gain back the power he'd lost, and keep rising.

"I looked. Couldn't…find it," he wheezed.

Brandon balled his hands into fists, battled the urge to let his hired muscle break a few more bones in that pathetic face. "You will."

He was going to make Greg suffer for what he'd done to him. Beginning with taking back everything that was stolen from him without his knowledge. While in prison he'd toyed with the idea of targeting Greg's parents, the wealthy philanthropists who'd created the ungrateful bastard before him now. But that would bring a shit ton of heat down on him and it was too risky when he was just beginning his climb back into the trade.

"Can't," Greg rasped.

His temper snapped. He marched forward and grabbed a handful of Greg's hair, yanked hard and jerked the asshole's head back. "You didn't think I'd find out what you'd done? That I'd forget while I rotted in the prison you helped put me in?" He shook his head, let Greg see the rage inside him. "I don't forget. Ever. So you're going to find what you took, and you're going to give it back to me." Then he'd die.

Greg's throat moved in a jerky motion as he swallowed, the stink of fear rolling off him in waves. "I don't know where it is," he insisted.

"Your ex will."

Those bruised, bloodshot eyes locked on his. "She doesn't…know anything."

"She'll know where the furniture is. I'm sure she could be…motivated to find it for me."

Greg scoffed and huffed out a dry laugh. "She doesn't know shit about what I did."

Maybe not, but Brandon could still use her. "Guess we'll find out, won't we?"

Greg glared up at him in defiance and managed a slight shrug. "There's no point going after her. She means nothing to me and it's not going to get you what you want."

The words sounded real enough, but Brandon caught the spark of fear in those deep blue eyes, and it told him everything he needed to know. The pathetic son of a bitch was lying through his teeth. Greg still loved her, was trying to protect her even now.

It was almost laughable. Everyone knew how his ex had up and bailed on his pathetic ass over a year ago.

Brandon had never imagined gaining leverage against him so easily, having such powerful leverage at his disposal.

Brandon released Greg's hair with a cruel jerk and stepped back, a hard, ruthless ball of anger forming in his gut. If he wanted to gain the attention and admiration of the top cartel members in DC, he had to up his game.

He'd never gone after innocents before, but he had no choice now. Not if he wanted to establish his reputation as a top contender. The organization was watching him; he needed to impress them and show that he was merciless enough to warrant bringing on board.

Greg's nostrils flared, a move that had to be painful considering his broken nose. "She's got nothing to do with this. Leave her alone. It's between you and me."

Brandon barked out a laugh. "You don't get to call the shots this time, asshole. You brought her into this. Whatever happens to her is on you." He was going to make an example out of them, as a warning of what happened to those who crossed him.

Leaving the prisoner to bleed and sweat in his seat, Brandon turned and walked away. "Think I'll leave you to think things over for a while," he threw over his shoulder. "Maybe when I come back you'll have figured out a way to get what I want."

He stepped past the man guarding the door and out into the hallway. His shoes were quiet against the tile floor, the air cool and smelling of cleaner instead of blood and sweat. In his world, power and money were the only currencies that mattered. Fear and respect were how you got them.

Brandon knew exactly what he would do.

He'd get back what was his, then kill the ex-wife in front of Greg before giving the bastard the death he'd earned.

Chapter FIVE

After helping his dad bring the horses in from the pasture and put them in the barn, Easton walked out to the nearest white rail fence and paused to stare out at the rolling fields beyond it. The pastureland spread across the property like a lush green carpet beyond the paddocks. They sloped down the hill, then disappeared into the acres of forest that banded three sides of the property, offering them total privacy.

Setting one booted foot on the lower rail, he braced his stacked forearms on the upper one and inhaled a deep breath of the cool morning air. Fall was definitely here, he could smell the sweet dampness of it and see it in the bright bursts of color forming in the distant trees. His favorite time in the Valley, and while he loved being home with his family, all he could think about was Piper.

He hated that she'd been dragged into more drama from Greg, and wished he could make it all go away for her. She'd been understandably emotional last night after seeing the mess and blood at her house, and though he'd loved to have comforted her, she'd clearly wanted to be alone so he'd given her space.

Then the cops had come to look through the shed with them. They'd found the dresser Piper thought Greg meant, but hadn't found anything in it that would explain his desperation.

He glanced behind him to check her window in the house, the need to see her pricking at him like sharp needles. She probably wasn't up yet because the blind was still down and it was still early. After all she'd been through yesterday, she needed a good sleep.

Tamping down his impatience, he walked across the lawn and the gravel border that surrounded the house. He opened the back door and stepped into the kitchen.

"Hey."

Startled, he whipped his head around. His sister Charlie walked toward him from the living room, coffee in hand. Her long, dark brown hair was drawn back into a low ponytail and she was dressed in sweats. She must have rolled right out of bed and headed for her car. "Hi. When did you get in?"

"About an hour ago. You guys were out in the barn. Where's Dad?"

"Out there with the farrier."

"He still does that? Hovers over the guy while he files down the horses' hooves?"

"Oh yeah. Die hard control freak, gotta love it. So why'd you drive out so early?"

She covered a yawn. "After you called last night and told me what was going on with Piper, I couldn't sleep, so I just decided to head out." She looked over at the staircase. "She still sleeping?"

"Think so."

His sister plunked herself into a chair at the long farmhouse table and rubbed at her eyes. "I hate that she's going through this crap again."

"I know."

The floorboards creaked overhead. They both looked up and a moment later Piper appeared on the top of the stairs, her honey-colored hair loose around her shoulders, dressed in snug jeans and a black sweater that hugged the plump mounds of her breasts. Her face brightened when she saw Charlie. "Hi!"

Charlie got up and enveloped her in a hug. Easton wished the hug and the smile were for him. "Hi, hon."

Several inches shorter than his sister, Piper leaned back to peer up at her. "What are you doing here?"

"I was planning to come down and spend the weekend anyway, but Easton called me last night and told me what happened."

"Oh." She stepped back and lowered her gaze to the floor. "You didn't have to do that."

Charlie snorted and gave her a hard look. "Uh, yeah I did. You'd do the same for me, right? So what's the difference when you need me?"

Piper sighed. "I just hate that I'm dragging everyone into this."

"You're not dragging anyone. In case you can't see, we've volunteered."

"And that's why I love you guys." A slight smile tugged at her mouth, then she looked Easton's way and a fine tension settled in her expression. What was that about? "Morning."

"Morning. Have a good sleep?"

"Pretty good, yes."

Liar. Her eyes were swollen and puffy and had dark circles beneath them. It bothered him that she'd been crying alone in her room last night. He'd have given anything for the chance to climb in bed beside her and hold her, make her feel safe and let her know she wasn't alone. He'd been damn tempted to do just that.

One step at a time. "Want some coffee?"

"Love some."

He filled a mug for her, added sugar and cream before handing it to her.

She smiled as she accepted it. "Thanks. Remember that time we all went camping together and you accidentally left the milk out of the cooler? You made us all coffee the next morning and it looked like you'd poured cottage cheese in there."

I remember everything *about you.*

But he most definitely didn't want her thinking about him as a fourteen-year-old kid. "Yeah, I had to ride my bike the eight miles into the nearest town to buy fresh stuff." He waited until they were all at the table with their coffee and a plate of toast before continuing. "I talked to Wyatt last night. He and Austen are going to meet us at your place around nine. They'll help us clean up and start repairs." The cops had called her last night to say her house was no longer a crime scene.

Piper's brow creased and she set her mug down. "Oh, but they already have so much work at—"

"Stop. They're coming, so that's that. They're good at what they do, and between the five of us we can put a serious dent into the repairs over the next few days. If all goes well, you can restage your place and start showing it again on Monday." Although part of him wanted it to take forever, so he'd get to spend more time with her—and so she wouldn't be able to sell and move away. "Austen said she'll be glad to take a look at the pie chest and let you know if she can fix it."

Her face brightened. "She did?"

"Yes, ma'am."

"Well, if they're sure and they don't mind taking time away from their own house…"

Easton exchanged a glance with Charlie and barely refrained from laughing when his sister rolled her eyes. As if there'd ever been any question that Wyatt and

Austen would jump in to help Piper.

Being on the receiving end of charity always made her uncomfortable, but in this case, too bad. There was no reason for her to go through this alone when she had all of them to back her up. Family took care of each other and he couldn't understand why she didn't seem to get that. She'd faced everything by herself far too often in the past, something he admired her for but also regretted. If he'd known what was really going on with her before, he'd have…

You'd have what? You've been on constant rotations overseas for the past two years.

Well, he would have done something. And his family would have as well.

After they ate he drove them all to Piper's place. She was quiet as they walked to the back door, then she squared her shoulders in a *let's do this* move that was classic Piper.

He knew this was hard on her. If they'd been alone he would have pulled her into a hug just to reassure her but Charlie would know it was more than concern, and he didn't want to tip his hand before he'd had a chance to talk to Piper about his feelings first.

"Holy shit," Charlie murmured when they walked into the kitchen and she saw the damage on the inside.

"Pretty much, yeah," Piper said, heading through the mudroom into the laundry room. "All the cleaning stuff is in here."

"I'll take the kitchen," he said. He didn't want Piper to have to deal with the blood.

"Okay. Thanks. I'll start in the family room." She handed him a bucket, mop and bottle of bleach.

"I'll help you," Charlie said, trailing after her with a broom and dust pail.

He got to work cleaning up the blood then disinfected the floor, wiped down all the cabinets and the countertops. In the middle of pouring the last of the red-tinged water down the sink, Wyatt and Austen showed up.

His eldest brother strode in through the back door without knocking, his gaze going straight to the bloody water in the bucket. The mass of scars on the right side of his face tightened. "You need help in here?"

"No, almost done. Worst of the damage is out front." He nodded in the direction of the family room.

Austen came in behind Wyatt, shot Easton a smile that made her silver-gray eyes sparkle, a stark and beautiful contrast to her light brown skin. She was tall, the same height as Easton, and solid muscle, a former firefighter and talented carpenter. She was awesome, and he was beyond thrilled that his brother had found her.

Truth was, he'd been worried as hell about Wyatt before Austen had shown up. They all had. That IED blast in Afghanistan had changed him into a completely different person, and not just because it had taken one eye and his lower leg. Wyatt had lost his military working dog as well as his men, and that kind of loss never went away.

Easton wasn't worried about him anymore though. That girl had Wyatt wrapped so hard around her diamond engagement ring-studded finger it wasn't even funny. Easton would have loved her forever for that alone, so it was just a bonus that he liked her anyway.

"Hey, handsome," she said to him.

"Hey." He grinned back at her. "Thanks for coming."

"Wouldn't miss it." She glanced around, her tight, dark curls bouncing around her shoulders as her head moved. "Wow."

"Pretty much, yeah."

"Where's the pie chest?"

He'd already explained to her over the phone last night how important it was to Piper. He hoped she'd be able to fix it. “Through there.” He pointed toward the sound of broken glass being swept up.

Austen walked through the kitchen and headed for where he’d indicated, but Wyatt hung back, leaning against the counter and crossing his arms over his massive chest. “She okay?” he murmured, staring at him with intense hazel eyes just like their father’s.

“Not sure. You know how she is. Strong, stubborn. Suffers in silence.” He hated that *so* much.

Wyatt nodded and clenched his jaw, making the scars twitch. “I knew that fucker wasn’t finished screwing with her yet.”

The show of protectiveness didn’t stir any jealousy in Easton. There was zero attraction between his brother and Piper. She was a Colebrook, plain and simple. Easton hoped to make that official someday, hopefully sooner rather than later. A ring on her finger, and not long after that, giving her his name. “Well, looks like he’s paying for it now.”

“Still no word on what happened to him?”

“Not yet. Hoping for an update sometime today. Come on, let’s go see how we want to tackle this.”

“Is the glass all cleaned up?”

“Think so.”

“Hang on, I’m gonna get Grits. Piper would like that.”

Yeah, she would. But as big and tough as Wyatt was, he wasn’t fooling anyone with that excuse. He was almost as attached to that dog as he was to Austen. Another miracle, considering Wyatt had vowed never to own another dog after Raider had been killed.

The start of the transformation had been all Piper’s doing. She’d known Wyatt since they were eighteen and had seen right through his miserable recluse act. Somehow she’d known the dog would force him to feel again, and had dropped Grits off on his doorstep without warning. She'd not only rescued Grits, but Wyatt too, and Easton would always be grateful to her for that.

Out in the family room the girls had cleaned up all the broken pictures and stacked them onto the now-righted coffee table. "The TV's a loss," Piper said in a discouraged voice.

"I can definitely do something with this pie chest though," Austen said, running her hand over the split in the rear of the now-righted chest, and the broken doors. "No guarantees I can make it as good as new, but it'll be close."

The sound of little paws on the hardwood made Piper turn her head. Her entire face lit up when she saw the dog trotting toward her, feathery white tail swishing, long brown ears flopping. "Grits!"

The Cavalier King Charles spaniel rushed over, tail wagging, his prosthetic right rear leg thumping on the floor. The asshole who had tried to kill Austen and Wyatt a few months ago had shot Grits. Little guy had lost a leg, but it hadn't slowed him down any.

Piper scooped him up and buried her face in his soft fur. "How's my little sweetheart doing, huh?" she crooned, kissing and cuddling him and basically turning the little guy into a puddle of mush in her arms.

Easton didn't blame him, although he wasn't proud of being jealous of a damn dog. What he wouldn't give to have her be that openly affectionate with him, hug and kiss him without reservation. He wanted all of her.

"He's doing great," Wyatt said, beaming like a proud father as he stood there grinning at them. "He told me he missed you so he wanted to come over too."

Piper snickered and looked up at him. "Uh-huh. And it has absolutely nothing to do with the fact that you can't bear to be apart from each other?"

"No, of course not."

Austen snorted. "Whatever. They're ridiculous.

Inseparable. I swear I don't know who's more in love with Wyatt, me or the dog."

Wyatt shrugged, his lips quirking. "What can I say, I'm just a loveable guy."

"Yeah you are," Austen said, and stepped over to plant a kiss on his lips. "Big softie."

Wyatt grimaced. "Not in front of everyone," he complained.

"Oh please, like it's any kind of secret to the rest of us," Piper said. Grinning, she kissed the brown spot on the top of Grits's head and set him down. The dog immediately went across the room to greet Charlie, then Easton.

"Any more pieces from your grandma here?" Easton asked Piper as he scratched Grits on the chest and lifted his chin to avoid the lizard-like tongue trying to lick him.

"Just a couple of prints that I now have to get reframed, and a jewelry box." She pushed to her feet. "There's nothing hidden in it. I emptied everything out of the furniture and packed it all in boxes before I put it in storage."

Was worth taking another look, just to make sure she hadn't missed something. When it came to searching for hidden contraband, Easton was an expert. He did it on pretty much every mission his team went on. "Can I see the box?"

"Sure." She led him into her bedroom and picked up the art deco jewelry box that had been dumped onto the floor. The air in here smelled faintly of her perfume. "All my jewelry is still here," she said, gathering up the earrings and necklaces strewn on the carpet. "It's weird. Greg and whoever attacked him couldn't be that hard up for money if he didn't take any of this, right?"

Just means whatever they're after is worth a whole lot more than your jewelry. "They weren't after jewelry." Her face fell and he changed the subject. "We should go down to your storage locker later and have a look at what you've got in there. After that we can check out the stuff in the shed at my dad's place. I'll help you."

"Okay." She continued gathering up her things from the floor. Jewelry, sexy lace bras and panties he'd fantasize about seeing her in from now on, and other odds and ends from the dresser. He picked up whatever he found and placed it on the bed for her to sort back into the drawers. Piper was obsessed about organization.

A few minutes in, her phone chimed. The insurance company, or maybe the cops? Easton only paid partial attention to her as he continued cleaning up the items on the floor but when she gasped he tensed and jerked his gaze to her.

"Oh my God," she whispered, her face full of horror, one hand flying up to cover her mouth.

Oh, shit, what now? "What is it?" he asked, stepping close to her.

Face so pale the freckles stood out on her nose, she handed over the phone without a word. Anger punched through him when he saw what the caller had sent. An image of Greg, bound to a chair with his hands secured behind him, face badly beaten. And below it, a chilling message.

Give us what we want or he'll die a slow, painful death.

Chapter SIX

"He was doing so well this time. Every time I spoke to him on the phone this past month, it was like talking to the old Greg. I really thought he was going to make it, that he would finally kick the addiction," Bea said with a sad little sniffle.

Piper rubbed at her forehead and sighed. Her ex-mother-in-law was in Paris right now with her husband and trying to deal with her son being held prisoner and possibly tortured while the police scrambled for leads. "Even if he was, the lifestyle wouldn't ever let him go," she said as gently as she could. They'd had this same conversation so many times before. "He's made too many enemies and burned too many bridges." Including every single one leading back to her.

A soft sob filled the line. "But he's been clean for nearly three months, the longest stretch ever. If he can kick the addiction, then he should be able to get his life back."

Bea spoke as a mother who loved her only child with

everything in her. She couldn't accept that her precious baby boy was lost to her forever. Piper had no such illusions. He had to hit rock bottom before he made a change, and he had to *want* to change. Piper wasn't sure he'd ever get there.

"I'm so sorry, Bea. The police are doing everything they can to find him." It had definitely been Greg's blood on her kitchen floor though. The hardest part had been telling Bea that the police had no idea who had taken him, or why. Though it had to be drug related.

"I can't believe this has happened. He was doing so well… I just feel sick, knowing what he's going through and that there's nothing we can do to help him, even when we get home."

"I know." Her relationship with her ex-in-laws had been strained since she'd left Greg, but they still loved her and in her own way, she loved them too. After all, Piper had worked her ass off for them for years, for nothing.

Shortly after she and Greg had gotten engaged, she'd left her teaching job to dive in and help out full time with all their charities, organizing galas and working on various boards of trustees. While she regretted leaving her job for her husband, she didn't regret the experience she'd gained from working with charitable foundations.

When she'd left Greg, she'd quit all that and turned to real estate to make money. His parents had been hurt, but they'd understood her decision. She needed distance from them and their world every bit as much as she did from Greg. Until the other day, she'd been well on her way to getting her life back and rediscovering who Piper Greenlee truly was.

"And whatever he was looking for—you'll keep searching for it, right? If you can find it, then maybe whoever kidnapped him will release him. Or maybe they'll ask for a ransom. We'll pay whatever they want if they'll let him go."

Piper hesitated before responding. Bea was an incredibly intelligent woman, so her comment had to be borne of desperation. She knew from Greg how ruthless the drug underworld was, and that the chances of Greg surviving this were pretty much nil, whether Piper found the missing item or not.

In the end, she simply didn't have the heart to extinguish that tiny flame of hope for her. She and Easton had already checked all her grandmother's furniture with the cops and found nothing, but it wouldn't hurt to look again. "I'll keep looking," she promised. Maybe they'd missed something. Even if she had nothing but contempt for Greg's behavior and what he'd put her through, she still didn't want to see him die and couldn't stand to see him suffer the way he was. If she could save his life, she would.

"Thank you," Bea breathed. "I guess this is partly our fault, isn't it? You were right. We loved him too much, tried to protect him when we shouldn't have. And now we have to live with that."

Piper cringed inside. "Are you guys flying home then?" she asked to change the subject.

"Tom booked us a flight first thing in the morning. The police are going to update us with any new findings when we get home tomorrow night, but if you hear anything sooner, will you let me know right away?"

"Yes, of course. Safe flight home."

"Thank you."

She ended the call and sat there alone on the Colebrooks' front porch swing for a long while, emotionally exhausted. Staring out across the huge expanse of lush green lawn that sloped away from the front of the house, she cleared her mind.

There was nothing more she could do for Greg at the moment, and nothing she could do to make her ex-in-laws feel any better. She had nothing to feel guilty about and again thought maybe it was a good idea to cut them out of her life entirely, because they were a reminder of Greg.

Pushing out a deep breath, she willed the lingering tension away. It was so peaceful out here, away from town. She'd spent so much time here at the house over the years. Thanksgivings, Christmases and Easters after her father died, and before she'd married Greg. This place felt more like home to her than anywhere else, yet some part of her still felt like an outsider, no matter how wonderful the Colebrooks had been to her.

Above her the night sky was a deep midnight blue, filled with thousands of twinkling stars. A cool breeze blew through the oak and cherry trees planted on either side of the house, rustling the changing leaves and rippling through the grass. A chorus of crickets and frogs hummed in the background, providing a soft lullaby that soothed her jangled nerves.

Inhaling the cool, clean fall air, she closed her eyes and tipped her head back to rest it on the top of the swing. It had been a bitch of a day.

After receiving that awful text, she'd spent hours talking with the detectives handling her case, then had cleaned and started repairs on the worst of the damage at her house. The insurance company had been great so far but she was glad Easton, Wyatt, Austen and Charlie had volunteered to help her because she was in a rush to get the house ready for showing and didn't want to wait for all the paperwork to be processed.

The front door opened with a slight creak. She lifted her head as Easton stepped out onto the front porch.

Her heart beat faster at the sight of him. He'd been with her all day, had barely left her side through all the police stuff, and he'd worked tirelessly with her at the house afterward. He made it harder and harder for her to ignore her growing attraction toward him, and she was afraid he would notice somehow.

"How'd it go?" he asked, walking toward her. Even the way he moved was sexy. Strong and confident, smooth.

Wyatt's little brother.

The reminder snapped her out of that line of thinking. "Bea's devastated. She kept saying that Greg was a changed man, that this round of rehab had finally set him straight." She shook her head.

"If wishes were horses," he murmured.

"Exactly."

He lowered his weight next to her on the swing. She tensed a little. He was so close she could smell the faint scent of his cologne, a sexy, evergreen scent, and had to resist the urge to edge away. "

You okay?" he asked, his warm brown eyes intent on her face as he laid an arm across the top of the swing's back, the heat of it wrapping around her shoulders.

It was torture, being this close to him and having to pretend she felt nothing more than friendship while her hormones went crazy and her body craved his touch. "Yes."

She refused to complain. Easton had busted his ass to get where he was in life. As a member of the world's most elite counter-narcotics team he risked his life on a daily basis whenever he went on a mission, or even during training. He regularly did four-month-long rotations to Afghanistan, one of the most dangerous places on earth, hunting down terrorists and drug smugglers with the threat of being wounded or killed hanging over him and his team every single minute.

So no, she wasn't going to whine about her current predicament.

"You sure you're ready to go back to work tomorrow?" he asked.

"Yes. I had to cancel all my appointments today."

She needed the money those house sales would earn her. When she left Sugar Hollow, she meant to do it debt free so she could relocate and begin anew. Her ex-in-laws had offered to pay it all off for her plenty of times, maybe out of guilt or obligation, she wasn't sure. Every time she'd turned them down because she didn't want to feel like she owed them anything. If she paid it all off herself, she could be free of the whole family once and for all.

"I'll go with you to the showings."

It came out a statement instead of an offer, but she didn't mind. With this craziness going on, she would feel more secure with him looking out for her. "Are you sure?"

"Of course I'm sure."

"Okay, then. Thanks."

"What time's the first one?"

"Eight, but it's not far from downtown. We could stop at the *Garden of Eatin'* on our way there, grab a bite first."

"Sounds good. We'll leave at seven?"

"Sure." She covered a yawn, giving her the perfect excuse to leave. "Well. Guess I'll turn in."

He stood and offered a hand. She took it and he pulled her to her feet, the feel of his strong hand around hers making something low in her belly flutter.

But he didn't let go. Instead he wrapped his arms around her back and pulled her into a hug.

When the initial surprise passed she sighed and leaned into him, rested her forehead on his chest for a moment, her hands on his taut waist. Then he pressed a kiss to the top of her head, and her heart squeezed. He'd been so sweet to her the past couple of days, she didn't know what she would have done without him. Being in his arms was killing her though.

Just as she began to pull away Easton splayed his hands across her back, keeping her close. Then he bent his head to nuzzle the sensitive spot at her temple, his beard a soft prickle against her skin.

Piper went rigid and her eyes flew open. Her heart lurched then shot into double time. That kiss felt…way too intimate. Way too far out of the friend zone for her comfort. His embrace was protective. Almost possessive.

Confused, sure she was reading this wrong, she tipped her head back to look up at him. In the warm glow of the overhead porch light, the expression on his face made her heart seize.

Intense. Hungry. The way a man looked at a woman just before he kissed her until her knees gave out.

Her pulse skipped as shock blasted through her. Before she could move, let alone process everything, he cupped the side of her face with one big hand.

She stopped breathing, stared up into his eyes for one heartbeat, two. Okay, admittedly it had been a while since she'd been with a man, but she was *not* misinterpreting that look.

Easton wanted her. And not just as a friend.

Her eyes widened in the instant it took for him to lean down and gently press his lips to hers. She gasped, a dangerous tide of hunger and need eroding the shock.

She told herself to pull away but couldn't move, and he shifted his grip to her jaw, kissing her more firmly. A slow, lingering kiss that set off a dangerous burst of heat deep inside her.

She jerked away and stared up at him, her heart hammering, emotions in total chaos.

Gazing down into her eyes, he swept a thumb over her chin in a gentle caress, the warmth of his breath ghosting across her damp lips. "You have no idea how damn long I've wanted to do that," he murmured.

Piper could only stare. *What. The. Hell.* "Easton…" She trailed off at the shocking, molten hunger burning in his eyes, her mouth going dry.

Holy shit.

"What?" he whispered.

At first she didn't know what to say, then everything came out at once. "But…what… I'm so much older than you."

He laughed softly. "Of all the things you could have said, that's the first one that came to mind?"

Her face heated, her brain struggling to catch up. "I'm six years older than you. And we've been friends forever."

"Five and three-quarters. And yeah, we have."

"I used to *babysit* you," she protested, aghast. This was wrong. So very wrong.

So why does it feel so damn good then?

He snorted, as if that didn't matter to him in the slightest. "My dad asked you to hang around the house while he and the others were at work, just to make sure I didn't burn the place down."

"Yeah, and the first day you came back with a broken arm after riding your bike into a ditch."

"Didn't burn the place down though, did I?"

This was too crazy. She shook her head, blurted out more. "We're too different. You date a lot of women and you're gone all the time with your job. And I used to date your *brother*." The last thought was so mortifying she stepped back and put her hands to her hot cheeks. Oh my God, what was wrong with her, lusting after Wyatt's little brother?

Easton lowered his hand and stood there watching her for a long moment. "I haven't seen anyone since long before I found out you were getting a divorce."

That stunned her. "You haven't?" Her voice sounded so small.

He shook his head. "No, because I don't want anyone but you." When she simply stared at him in stunned silence, he continued. "Does the rest of that stuff really matter to you? Yeah, I'm gone a lot with my job and I can't help that, but I'm hoping that doesn't put me out of the running."

Out of the running? With *her*? This was too bizarre. She barely resisted the urge to run past him and upstairs to hide in Charlie's room.

"As for you and Wyatt, you guys dated a hundred years ago, for just a couple weeks. It wasn't serious, and you never slept together."

She nearly choked. "You asked him that? Back *then*? You were thirteen!" There was no way he could have had those kinds of feelings for her back then.

"Yeah. And I was insanely jealous of Wyatt for a long time after you guys broke up, because I had a serious crush on you, even back then. I told him then that I thought he was the dumbest shit in the universe for letting you go, but I'm glad you guys broke up when you did."

She couldn't even believe what she was hearing. It was so hard to accept what he was saying, his words throwing her entire world off kilter. "You mean…all along, all this time…?"

He nodded once, his eyes somber. "But especially the past ten years or so."

Ten years. Oh my God.

She took a step backward, reached behind her to feel for the porch swing because her legs were about to give out. She sat with an ungraceful plop and stared at him, feeling like she was seeing him for the first time.

And what a view it was, his tall, muscular form silhouetted by the porch light. He was the kind of man who could have any woman he wanted. Yet he wanted her, and had for more than a decade? Did she understand that right?

"I had no idea," she managed, trying to ignore the way her body was going haywire. It was forbidden. She couldn't act on it. Wouldn't.

"Yeah, I noticed." His voice held an ironic edge.

Bewildered, she shook her head. "You never gave a single indication that you were interested in me before now."

"Yeah, because by the time I was old enough for you to see me as something besides Wyatt's little brother, you were engaged. And then you got married."

Her heart was racing, her body caught in a wild mix of euphoria and disbelief. "Wow," was all she could say.

He sat next to her again but didn't crowd her this time, leaving a space between them, and he didn't try to touch her. She appreciated that he didn't push because she was struggling to make the mental adjustment between friends and way more than friends and one more move from him would have sent her running.

"So have I read you wrong?" he asked. "Is it just one-sided on my part?"

Her face flamed hotter. There was no way she was going to admit her change of feelings toward him right now. "We can't."

"Why not?"

"Because we're friends, Easton."

"And us being together is going to change that?"

"It could," she fired back. It probably would. And if anything went wrong, she risked losing not just him, but her surrogate family as well. "It could ruin everything." God, she wished he'd never kissed her or told her any of this.

"I know this is a shock to you," he allowed, "but I would never do anything to jeopardize—"

"I'm moving to Minnesota," she said in desperation, trying to get through to him. This would never work.

They were too different, and their lives weren't compatible.

"If that's what you really want, if the job means that much to you, then we'll work it out."

He wasn't listening. "You're the wild child of the family. I'm straight-laced and that's not going to change." How would that even work between them?

He gave her a slow smile that made hot tingles explode in her abdomen. "I've grown up a lot over the years, in case you haven't noticed. Not nearly as wild as I used to be. Any other objections?" He took her hand, curled his long, strong fingers around hers.

"You're just going to shoot them down one by one no matter what I say, aren't you?" she said in exasperation, every nerve ending in her body clamoring for his touch.

"Yes, ma'am. So. What else you got?" He settled back against the porch swing. "I'm ready. Shoot."

It was impossible to think clearly with him touching her, even just her hand. All she could focus on was what it would be like to shed her inhibitions and go for the opportunity he'd offered. To give into the guilty cravings she'd indulged in over the past few months.

Her gaze strayed to the windows at the front of the house, mind racing. "What about your family? It would be so weird for them." Yeah, she was grasping at straws now, but she was desperate to make him see reason and cringed at the thought of making things awkward for his family.

"Don't care if it was, but no, I think after the initial surprise, they'd be happy for us. And I know you, so I know you're already worrying about what other people in town will say. Don't. I don't care what anybody else thinks except you. All that matters is whether you feel anything for me beyond friendship. I know I've dated a lot of women in the past, but none of them mattered to me."

She met his gaze again, heart thudding, damn near holding her breath as she waited to hear what he said next.

With gentle fingers he brushed a lock of hair away from her cheek, skimmed his fingertips over the edge of her face, the touch light as a sigh but she felt it all the way to her bones. "Because none of them were you. And once I found out you were single last time I was home, you were all I could think about. I'm not interested in anyone else. I only want you."

Jesus.

Her pulse drummed in her ears, his words echoing in her head. She was terrified to admit she wanted him too, but he was experienced enough to know that her reaction to the kiss had already told him the truth. *Crap.* "We just can't," she whispered finally, stricken.

Rather than get upset, one side of his mouth lifted in a sexy grin that made her toes curl in her flip-flops. He cupped the side of her face again, leaned in to brush a gentle kiss over her parted lips. "Just sleep on it."

With that he pushed up from the swing and went into the house as though nothing out of the ordinary had happened, when in reality he'd just turned her entire world upside down.

Piper closed her eyes and buried her face in her hands. She was in hell. The sooner she sold her place and left Sugar Hollow, the better.

Chapter SEVEN

"Piper Greenlee. She went back to her maiden name when she left him."

Brandon nodded and poured himself a few inches of vodka over some ice. In prison he'd been denied every luxury and he planned to make up for lost time. "That's what I figured. What else?" He hadn't been able to dig into Greg's ex-wife's life until now because he'd been in jail until just a few days ago, so he had his guys out doing it for him.

"She's a local real estate agent. Word is she's been spotted around town with this guy since yesterday."

Brandon took the man's phone and stared at the photo. Recognition flared in his gut. He knew that face. Brandon had seen him before, just couldn't place him. "What's his name?"

The man blinked at him. "You know him?"

Brandon nodded. "Don't know from where. Who is he?"

"Easton Colebrook."

Colebrook… Something sparked in his memory. Images swirled through his brain like a movie on fast forward. Of the night of the sting when he'd been arrested. A cop? "What have you got on him?"

"His dad has a big spread of property outside of town. Horse farm. Well-respected family. Three sons, one daughter, and the old man had a stroke a few years ago. He and the sons all served in the Marines."

Brandon stared at the picture, frustration building inside him. He knew he'd met this man the night of his arrest.

He sucked in a breath as recognition hit him. "He's a fucking DEA agent."

The man's eyebrows shot up. "What? Are you sure?"

"Yeah, I'm fucking sure. I met him during a deal two weeks before I was busted, didn't realize he was an undercover agent. Christ. I didn't find out who he was until I talked to another guy in the joint who'd been arrested that same night." He shoved the phone back at him and paced away, dragged a hand through his hair. "What the hell's she doing with a DEA agent?"

"I don't know, but we've been working on his profile all afternoon and haven't found shit."

"Because his info is classified, obviously," Brandon muttered. Hell, this was more complicated than he'd imagined. "How close is she to him?"

The man shrugged. "From what I can tell, she's just a friend of his family."

"Nothing more to it?"

"Don't think so."

Didn't feel right to Brandon. Greg's ex suddenly hanging with the same DEA agent who had brought Brandon down? Way too much of a coincidence. "Any chance he's dirty? Can we get him for the right price?"

"Doubtful. From what I heard, the Colebrooks are pillars of the community-type people."

Brandon shot him a sideways glance. "Sheriff Greg Rutland used to be too."

"True, but if she's a friend of the family, Colebrook's not gonna turn on her or risk her safety."

"Where is she staying?"

"We don't know yet. We're checking local hotels, but she may be staying with relatives or friends. Possibly the Colebrooks."

He spun around and aimed a lethal glare at the guy. "Find her."

"Yessir," he murmured, lowering his eyes before he turned and rushed from the room.

Brandon tamped down his anger and absorbed the stillness surrounding him. A goddamn undercover DEA agent. It was almost funny. Except it wasn't.

But maybe…maybe there was a silver lining here.

He strode through the mansion's game room and out through the leaded glass French doors that led onto the back patio. The large, rectangular-shaped pool glowed a bright turquoise in the darkness. Tall, wrought-iron lamp posts ringed the flagstone patio, casting pools of yellow light over the neatly trimmed boxwood hedges surrounding the private backyard, and the lush green grass of the lawn.

An old trafficker friend had loaned him the place for the next week, if he stayed that long. This place suited Brandon. When he made it into the upper echelons of the cartel, he was going to have a place even better than this. Somewhere out of the States, maybe in the Caribbean or Mexico. He would live like a fucking king, and no one would dare cross him. He'd be rich enough to buy his freedom, even from the goddamn DEA.

He needed to beef up the plan he'd devised while behind bars, and capitalize on this opportunity. If he killed Colebrook in addition to Greg and the ex-wife, it would be one hell of a statement. Everyone would see he wasn't intimidated by the feds or any other government agency.

That kind of coup would satisfy his need for revenge in addition to salvaging his reputation. It might even propel him into a nice position of power within the cartel once word of what he'd done spread to the right people.

He sipped at the vodka, enjoying the mellow burn as it slid down his throat. "Go wake up our prisoner," he said to the other man standing watch out on the deck. This time he wasn't taking chances with his personal security. "Find out what he knows about Colebrook." There had to be an opportunity here. He'd kill three birds with one stone, rather than two.

Easton Colebrook was now in his crosshairs. Brandon was going to make sure the DEA agent died with the other two.

****

Easton let out a deep exhale and walked through the cabin's living room out to the screen porch with a mug of coffee. It was still dark out, the first streaks of light barely visible over the tops of the Blue Ridge Mountains. He loved this quiet time before the sun came up. Overseas, darkness meant danger. Here at home, it meant peace and a chance to gather his thoughts.

The familiar sound of Wyatt's truck pulling up out front minutes later signaled that his reprieve was over. He wandered back into the kitchen as both Wyatt and Charlie stepped onto the front porch. He'd asked both of them here so he'd only have to say this once.

"Hey," he said, pushing the screen door open for them both. "Thanks for coming."

"You got coffee on?" Charlie asked, rubbing at her eyes. She was definitely not a morning person.

"Just made a fresh pot." He went to the coffee maker

and poured them each a mug while his siblings sat at the small kitchen table.

"So," Wyatt asked, cradling the mug between his big hands. "What was so important that you had to talk to both of us in person before the sun came up?"

"I have to fill you guys in on something." And given last night, it couldn't wait.

"Okay…" Charlie said, eyeing him with curiosity as she blew on her coffee. "So spill."

They were both sitting down, so he might as well just go for it. "It's Piper."

"Something else happen?" Wyatt asked in concern.

"Not with the investigation, no. This is about me and her."

Two pairs of eyes, one hazel and one deep brown, focused on him intently. "What about you guys?" Charlie asked, her expression suspicious.

"I'm gonna do whatever it takes to make her mine."

Charlie's mouth opened in shock and Wyatt's eyebrows first shot upward, then crashed together in a foreboding scowl. "What the hell do you mean?" he growled out, his protective reaction exactly what Easton had expected, but it also meant that Wyatt didn't trust Easton's intentions.

He tamped down his annoyance and raised a hand in self-defense. "I love her."

His brother and sister stared at him as a taut silence hummed between them.

"I've loved her a damn long time. When I came home this past spring and found out she was single, I made up my mind that I was going to make my move next time I was back."

"Um, okay, wow," Charlie said, face blank with surprise. "Does she have any idea you feel this way about her?"

"She does now." He'd shocked her pretty bad last

night but he hadn't been able to keep his feelings buried any longer.

"And?"

"And…I'm hoping she'll give us a chance, once she has time to think it over."

"So this is serious, right?" Wyatt asked, his scowl now mellowed to a puzzled frown, in full concerned big brother mode. "You love her, and you're going after her because you want…what?"

"It's as serious as it gets. She's it for me."

At that both his siblings gawked at him. He sighed. "Yeah, I know this comes as a surprise to you guys. It did to her too."

"Well no kidding," Charlie remarked dryly, her dark eyes now gleaming with excitement.

"That's why I wanted to tell you guys up front. She's got certain…reservations, I guess you'd call them, about us being together. On top of that, Greg did a number on her self-esteem and she hates that she's been the topic of town gossip for so long. She's hell bent on moving to Minnesota for her dream job teaching at a private school."

Charlie nodded. "This whole thing has been so hard on her. Piper's strong, but it's worn her down and she's just started to find her footing again. It's why she wants to start fresh elsewhere."

"Well I'm gonna do everything I can to convince her to stay," Easton said. "I laid most of my cards on the table for her last night."

"Wait, wait. What do you mean, *most* of your cards?"

"I may have left out the L word. Didn't want to freak her out completely and scare her off for good right out of the chute."

"Yeah, I guess I can see your reasoning on that one." Charlie set her mug down and leaned forward to rest her forearms on the table, her eyes intent on his. Worried, but hopeful. "So what did she say?"

"All the things I just said, plus she brought up our age difference, and her concern that anything romantic between her and I might wreck her relationship with the family." He shrugged, still hoping she'd get over that part.

"And you said…?" Charlie prompted.

"I think it's an excuse, so I told her to sleep on it and left it at that."

His sister groaned and closed her eyes. "Seriously?"

Easton's face started to heat up. "She was in shock. I wanted to give her time to process it and think things over without any pressure from me. I'm only telling you guys about it because I know she'll be worried about what you think and I don't want that to get in the way. I need you both to give us space while we figure this out," he added, a slight edge to his voice.

Charlie sighed and picked up her coffee while Wyatt continued to study him from across the table. "So did she seem receptive to the idea of you two together, or not?" his brother asked.

He grimaced. "She was pretty dead set about not being willing to go there." God, he hoped he'd be able to change her mind. He didn't know what he'd do if he couldn't. "But you guys know that no matter what she decides about us, I'm standing with her through this mess. I'll protect her either way, with everything I have."

Wyatt's frown disappeared and Charlie's lips curved in an approving grin. "Oh my God, you really are in love with her," she murmured.

"Yeah. If I had my way, I'd move her into my place in Alexandria right now. Permanently. But I guess she's not quite ready for something like that yet," he added with a sheepish grin.

Wyatt shook his head. "This isn't at all what I

expected you to tell us this morning," he said, taking a sip of his coffee, amusement in his eyes. "I knew you had a thing for her for a long time, but I never realized it ran this deep. I hope things work out for you."

The pressure in his chest eased slightly. It shouldn't have surprised him that Wyatt had picked up on it. "Thanks. Me too."

"Gonna be weird for the first little while," Charlie said. "If you guys do get together, I mean. She's been like a sister to us all for like, almost twenty years."

"Not to me," Easton said. "Not ever." Hell, he didn't know if things were going to turn out in his favor or not, but he'd been dying to tell her how he felt and was glad he'd finally put it out there last night. Well, most of it anyway.

"Well then. Hope she gives you a chance." Charlie's eyes filled with sympathy. "But try to remember how bad she's been hurt, Easton. She's not going to trust a man easily after what she went through, not even you, and if she's always seen you as just a friend or a brother before now… Be patient with her."

"I'm trying. It's why I decided to tell her last night and then give her space to think. I don't want to pressure her but I'm also not gonna stand back and let her walk away from me without a fight."

Wyatt nodded in approval, something that wasn't easily earned from his gruff eldest brother. "And what about her security situation? Have the cops found anything else yet?"

"No, and she insisted on starting work again today. I'll be going with her to all her appointments and showings. What do you think in terms of a timeline to finish the repairs on her place? Another day or two?"

"That should be plenty. I'm just waiting for the patches in the drywall to finish drying so I can sand and then paint. Austen's almost done with the repairs on the furniture. You said you're going to take care of buffing out the worst of the scratches in the hardwood floor, and all that's left after that is to clean and stage the place. Which we all know Piper will see to personally."

Easton smiled. Piper loved that kind of thing and would never let anyone else handle it. "Well, now that you know what's up, I'd appreciate it if you guys would make yourselves scarce around here for a while." His gaze strayed to the window next to the front door and out to the main house before looking back at his siblings. "I'm not sure what to expect from her this morning, so I'd like to have some time alone with her. I have a feeling she's going to either avoid me, or try to pretend last night didn't happen."

"Sure, no problem." Charlie looked at Wyatt. "Can I come by your place in a bit then? I'll go visit with Austen until we start work at Piper's place."

"Sure, yeah."

Easton saw them both out. Wyatt clapped him on the shoulder. "Good luck with everything."

"Thanks."

Charlie wrapped him up in a tight hug he returned. "Remember what I said. She's going to be skittish with anyone now. Don't take it personally."

"I won't."

After they left he closed the door and geared up for the coming challenges the day would bring. Piper was going to fight this, he was pretty sure.

Fortunately for him, he was a professional warrior. Even if she pulled away, he wasn't giving up. Piper was worth fighting for and he would do everything in his power to win her heart.

Chapter EIGHT

Okay, she couldn't stay up here forever. Sooner or later she had to go downstairs and face the day.

Piper pushed a hand through her shower-damp hair and took a calming breath. After a few restless hours last night spent staring at the ceiling and trying to figure out where to go from here, she'd somehow dropped off into a long, dreamless sleep.

Now that she was up and dressed, she had to face the music. Because no matter how much she wanted to avoid them, the situation with Greg and the new development with Easton had to be dealt with.

Outside the window the sun touched the edge of the mountain with brushstrokes of gold and orange, and birdsong filled the air. A perfect fall morning on a picturesque property in the middle of one of the most gorgeous places on earth. Except her heart and mind were in chaos.

Greg's kidnapping was enough to deal with, but the bombshell Easton had dropped on her last night had left her reeling. All this time she'd been friends with him, she'd had no idea he'd felt that way about her.

Now she was torn, and his admission had awakened a whole new level of need and forbidden thoughts about him. Maybe her physical attraction to him had been growing, but that didn't mean she was ready to act on it. She *couldn't* act on it. The prospect of getting involved with him romantically was definitely another disaster in the making.

As tempted as she was in some respects, she didn't see how this could end in any other way but heartbreak for her. She'd already taken the job in Minnesota and she wasn't prepared to give that up for anyone.

His life was here in Virginia. His family was solidly rooted here in Sugar Hollow, the one place she was desperate to escape from. If she gave into temptation and if things ended badly when she left, she would lose one of her dearest friends and make staying in contact with the rest of his family awkward for everyone.

And yet, as strong as all those arguments were to turn him down, none of them stopped her from wanting him.

She let out a groan of frustration and rubbed a hand over her face, dreading seeing him again, but it couldn't be helped and the sooner she dealt with it, the better. After putting on mascara, liner and lip-gloss, she gathered her courage and went downstairs to face him.

It wasn't Easton she found in the kitchen, however. It was Charlie.

Her friend smiled in greeting as she rinsed out a cup in the sink, dark brown waves spilling over her back. "Morning. You look fresh and rested. Feeling better?"

Not even a little. "Yeah, amazing what a good night's sleep will do for a girl." *I was up all night fantasizing about your brother.* She cringed inside, feeling dirty. God, she was nothing but a pervy cougar. The shame of it made her cheeks go hot.

Charlie shut off the water and reached for the kitchen towel hanging on the oven door handle to dry her hands, her deep brown gaze intent on Piper. “So, uh… Easton just told Wyatt and me about what he said to you last night.”

She let out a soft gasp, feeling like she’d just been sucker punched, and stood there feeling self-conscious as she tried to think of something to say. “Oh,” was all she came up with. Why the hell would he have told them that?

“I wasn’t supposed to say anything, but you’re one of my best friends and I thought you should know. We were both pretty surprised.”

Uh, yeah. “Well then that makes three of us.”

Charlie tipped her head to the side and crossed her arms over the plaid flannel shirt she wore. “Just so you know, he’s dead serious about you.”

Piper resisted the urge to squirm and rub a hand over the back of her tightening neck. “I really don’t know what to say.”

“You don’t have to say anything. I just wanted you to know, in case you didn’t believe him. I know you’ve been through a lot and that he took you off guard last night, but I’ve never seen him like this. I don’t want either of you to get hurt.”

“Nothing’s going to happen between us, Charlie. I’ll be leaving for Minnesota soon,” she said, as if that explained everything. “I already took the job, so my mind’s made up.”

Charlie’s eyes filled with sympathy. “We’ll all miss you when you go.” She hugged Piper and stepped back with a sunny smile, then changed the subject. “I’m heading out to Wyatt’s for a bit, but we’ll see you at your place later, once you’re finished with your showings.”

Piper nodded, dreading seeing Easton and being

alone with him in between appointments today. She owed him an answer, but didn't want to hurt his feelings and couldn't bear to break his heart. Had to be done though. She'd just do it as gently as possible and do whatever she could to salvage the friendship.

"Thanks. You guys don't know what it means to me to have friends like you."

"Yeah we do, we have you."

After Charlie left, Piper glanced at the window above the farmhouse sink and spotted Easton walking toward the house from the barn. Her heart did a funny little roll at the sight of him in a worn pair of jeans and a button-down chambray blue shirt with the sleeves rolled up to expose his thick forearms.

When she'd first moved here from Minnesota he'd been an awkward, gangly teenager. A wild, annoying kid with a bratty attitude and a penchant for irritating the hell out of her. She'd been the victim of more than her fair share of his practical jokes.

Well, there was nothing remotely awkward or bratty about the man he'd become. He moved with the confidence of a man who knew exactly who he was, and was comfortable with himself. She used to know how that felt.

Piper blew out a long breath as she watched him walk toward the house. To be honest, she'd spent a good portion of the night wrestling with the whole taboo, perving-on-Wyatt's-little-brother thing, and was mostly at peace with that part now that the initial shock of it all had worn off. He was a grown man and she was a grown woman. There was nothing to feel guilty about simply because she was attracted to him now.

Not that she had any intention of acting on those feelings. Of course she loved him, she'd known him for almost twenty years. She adored him and he meant the world to her, but there was no way she would jeopardize everything by crossing the line with him from friends to lovers.

She no longer trusted her judgment where matters of the heart were concerned. He'd laid a lot on the line with her last night, without spelling out exactly what he wanted from her. She'd been too afraid to ask him for details.

Anxiety clamped around her stomach like a vise as he pushed open the back door and stepped inside, his gaze locking with hers. A warm, sexy smile curved his mouth, making her pulse accelerate. "Hey. You ready to go?"

"Yes, just let me grab my purse." She spun away and went to retrieve it from the little table in the foyer, ordering herself to calm down. They were going to be together for most of the day and if she didn't figure out a way to fight these nerves, she was going to be a wreck before lunch.

Not wanting to get too close, she stepped past him when he held the back door for her and walked out to his truck. He jogged ahead and beat her to the passenger door, opened that for her too.

"Thanks," she murmured, not looking at him as she slid into her seat. God, she couldn't even look at him without triggering a chaotic mix of emotions.

Her stomach muscles tensed as he started the engine and headed down the driveway, the tension inside her building to the breaking point. They couldn't avoid the talk forever. She fully expected him to bring up last night and ask her for an answer, so his next words were a surprise.

"You still want to stop at the café first?"

Relief flooded her, and the pressure around her lungs eased. He was giving her a reprieve and she was grateful. "Sure. I'm starving."

"Me too. Wyatt figures it'll only be another day or two before you can start showing your house again."

At that, she looked over at him. "Really?"

He nodded. "And Austen's working her magic on the pie chest, so you'll have that back as well."

She swallowed to ease the sudden tightness in her throat. Was this wanting ever going to go away? "You guys are all so good to me."

"It's what friends do for each other," he said with a shrug.

But I don't know if I can be just your friend anymore. Now that he'd made her seriously contemplate the idea of being with him, she couldn't stop thinking about it, and every time she did, her body tingled all over.

She let herself stare at him a moment longer as he drove, admiring the lines of his profile, the strong jaw softened by the beard he'd trimmed, the straight blade of his nose. His features matched the solidity of his character.

Now that she knew how he felt about her and her mind kept conjuring up erotic images of them together, could she really walk away? Move a thousand miles away and maybe never see him again?

You have to. You know you do.

"You know, if it wasn't for the investigation going on, I'd have you out of this town so fast." He shook his head once.

The protectiveness behind the words made her melt inside. "Yeah, I need to stay close by in case the detectives need to meet with me."

"You got any plans for tonight, after work?"

She braced herself. "No, why?"

"I was thinking we could maybe go for a ride later."

She blinked. "You mean on horseback?"

The corner of his mouth tipped upward. "Yeah. When's the last time you went riding?"

"I don't even know. Couple years at least."

He shook his head. "Now that's a crime. You used to

love it."

"I still love it. It's just that life got in the way."

"So will you go with me later?" he asked, shooting her a sideways glance.

He wasn't exactly pressuring her about last night, though she was sure he'd bring it up at some point today. Maybe out on the ride. Escaping the craziness of late for a few hours sounded like heaven though.

"Love to," she said before she could talk herself out of it.

"Good," he answered, and there was just a hint of smugness in his grin.

The light conversation and prospect of a ride later erased most of her anxiety. It felt almost like old times.

By the time they got to the *Garden of Eatin'*, she wasn't nervous at all. In fact, she was more intrigued than anything else, and even let herself briefly imagine what it would be like to give into temptation. And the strangest part was, the longer he went without saying anything about last night, the more she wanted to talk about it.

After they ate, Easton took her to the first house on her list of showings. He swept the house and property before letting her inside, then stood in the front entryway when her clients arrived. He stayed put the whole time, even while she was talking to the couple in the kitchen at the end of the tour, a solid, steady presence there to protect her.

Despite herself, she kept stealing glances at him, admiring the long, powerful lines of his body as he kept watch. That strong, sexy and protective man was hers for the taking, if she allowed herself to.

The thought made her restless as hell. He was standing right there, within reach, and he wanted her. In a way that scared and intrigued the hell out of her.

Her heart beat faster just imagining what it would be

like to walk up to him and kiss that sinful mouth. To feel those big, strong hands moving over her body, chasing away the loneliness and isolation of the past few years.

"I like the house, but there are still a lot of things I'd want to change and that would put us above our budget," her female client said. "I've written a list of notes for later when we compare properties. Can we see the next one now?"

"Sure. You can follow us there."

She showed them three more places in the Sugar Hollow area, then one fifteen miles outside it. After the clients left the last house, Easton made her stay inside while he checked his truck as a precaution because he hadn't been able to keep a visual on it from the back of the house where Piper had talked with the couple. As she watched out the front window he paused, then went completely still, and his lips moved in an unmistakable curse.

"What's wrong?" she asked, hurrying out the door and down the front steps.

He met her at the back of the pickup and took her elbow. "Get in," he said, his clipped tone making her heart beat faster.

She did as he said, waited while he climbed in and started the engine. "Found this under the front bumper," he said, opening his right hand to show a small metal circle about the size of a watch battery in the center of his palm.

"What is it?"

"Tracking device," he said.

Her eyes widened. "What?"

"Someone's been following us."

"Out here?" They were miles away from Sugar Hollow. She glanced around nervously, seeing nothing but quiet sidewalks and driveways up and down both sides of the street. "For how long, do you think?"

"Don't know, but someone must have planted it at the last place. My guess is when we were checking out the acreage behind it. Dammit, I should have checked before."

That was already a few hours ago now. "But there's no way they could have found us unless they've been following us for a while."

He nodded once, jaw tight. "Yeah."

Piper wrapped her arms around her ribs and stared through the windshield, suddenly chilled. "Do you see anyone suspicious?"

"No. I'm betting they're long gone anyway. They wouldn't have expected me to look for, let alone find the tracker, so they probably assume we're oblivious and think they'll be able to follow us electronically."

An even more disturbing thought occurred to her. "What if they've been following us before this? What if they know I've been to your dad's place?"

"It's okay," he said calmly. "We'll handle it.

She was horrified. "God, I'm sorry—"

"Stop." The sharp tone made her go silent. "This isn't your fault. It's Greg's, and whoever the asshole is who took him." He used his hands free device to call Wyatt, then his father, and updated them. "Just keep an eye out and call me if you see anything suspicious. We're on our way to the police station to drop off the tracker. Piper's gonna have to cancel her remaining showings and then we'll be home."

She shook her head as he ended the call. "I can't go to your dad's place again, not if they know I've been there."

"We'll talk to the cops first, see what they say."

"I won't put you guys at risk. I'll find a hotel or—"

"No." Before she could argue further he reached across the console and took one of her hands, closed his fingers around it in a firm grip. "If they're following you then anywhere you go you'll be at risk. At least at our place you'll have me, Charlie and my dad to look out for you. Maybe Wyatt, too, if he wants to stay for a few days."

"But—"

"No buts," he said, squeezing her hand once before bringing it to his lips and pressing a quick, reassuring kiss to the back of her knuckles. "We'll go to the cops, then you're coming home with me."

Chapter NINE

Hours later, Easton swiveled atop his horse to look behind him, and smiled. Piper was a dozen yards away and closing in at a trot on the gentle mare he'd just saddled for her. "Stirrups okay?"

"Yes, perfect," she called back.

He reined his horse to the edge of the trail so she could come up alongside him, admiring the sight of her in the saddle. It had been too long since he'd been on horseback and it felt damn good to be out riding. And he could see Piper relaxing, so this had been the perfect idea to help her escape and steal some time alone with her.

The investigation on Greg had stalled. Even the Feds had no further leads. They were trying to trace the tracking device to find out who had planted it, but so far they hadn't been able to find prints or an origin for it.

When he'd first found it he'd been tempted to ask Charlie to see if she or her team of computer wizards could trace it, but had opted to take it to the cops because he wanted to cooperate fully with the locals.

Greg might be a fuck-up, but he was still the former sheriff and the locals wanted to get him back alive. They were more motivated to find him than anyone else assigned to the case. While Easton didn't much care if Greg came back alive, his death would upset Piper and that was reason enough to want him found safe.

Piper slowed her mount to a walk as she came up beside him. She looked so damn pretty with her hair loose around her shoulders and the touch of pink in her cheeks from the cool bite to the air, her round breasts bouncing ever so slightly with the horse's gait.

Did she have any idea how hard it had been for him to keep his hands off her all day? Watching her strut around earlier in those sexy heels and the snug pencil skirt suit that showed off her ass and legs had been torture. That and not bringing up last night had just about killed him. He didn't think she understood how much she affected him.

They rode across the northern pastures and through the woods bordering the far end of the property, then through the swinging gate and continued on the trail into county-owned land.

Gradually the groves of oaks and maples gave way to grassland that sloped down the hill, where the creek ran over the rocks through the glade in the hollow. The gentle rush of water grew louder as they approached the spot he'd picked out, and soon the creek came into view, meandering through the trees and into the pasture beyond.

"Oh, it's so beautiful," Piper breathed.

He glanced over at her in surprise, finding her far more beautiful than the scenery. "Never been out here before?"

"No. I've always just stayed on your property before."

This might not technically be Colebrook land anymore, but it might as well be. This place was secluded and in all the times he'd been out here, he'd never seen another soul.

"It's my favorite spot." He'd imagined bringing her out here so many times, he could hardly believe she was finally here alone with him. "Hungry?"

"Mmm, yes."

He was hungry for a lot more than the picnic they'd brought, but he'd have to see how things went. Much as he wanted her, he didn't want to push her if she wasn't ready for more. His sister was right, Piper was wary, might bolt if he made a wrong move. He couldn't risk screwing this up, no matter how badly he wanted her.

"Let's stop here," he said, halting his mount and swinging down from the saddle while she did the same.

He tethered the horses' reins to a low-hanging tree branch and left them to snooze while he unpacked the blanket and food from his saddlebags. Piper took the blanket from him and spread it out on the grassy bank of the creek.

His gaze immediately fixed on the round shape of her ass in those dark jeans as she bent over on her hands and knees to smooth out the wrinkles. Blood surged to his groin as he imagined peeling off her clothes and gripping her naked hips while he took her from behind.

She sat up and looked over her shoulder at him, tucking her hair behind her ear. "What?"

"Nothing." He'd caught the way she watched him when she thought he wasn't looking today, the secret longing in her eyes. God, he'd give anything for the chance to satisfy every last fantasy she had about him.

"No, what?"

Since he couldn't tell her what he was really thinking, he told her something else. "I was just thinking about when Wyatt came home from the hospital. I don't think

I've ever said it to you before, but one of the things I love most about you is how much you care about people. I'll never forget the way you were with Wyatt when he was recovering from all the surgeries."

She'd helped nurse him with the rest of them, run errands, cooked, cleaned, sat quietly with Wyatt when his depression was at its worst, and then kicked him in the ass when he needed a push later on. After that, she'd even stuck by Greg.

"He's my friend," she said simply. "Well, more like a brother."

"That's when you won my heart for good," he said, to make it clear he didn't think of her in any way as a sibling.

She met his gaze, and the gentle smile she gave him told him his words had touched her. "Was it my gentle bedside manner while I was changing his bandages, or yelling at him later when he was being an asshole to everyone?" she teased.

He chuckled. "Both. Not too many people I know can withstand the full force of Wyatt's temper, but you did. All five-feet-five-inches of you." He admired her so much for that. For her loyalty and compassion.

Because he was tempted to grab her and kiss each and every freckle on her nose and cheeks, he instead knelt on the other side of the blanket and set out the food they'd bought on their way back from the police station. A roasted chicken, bread, butter, cheese, some of the last peaches of the season and cream puffs filled with sweetened whipped cream and dipped in chocolate.

By the time he'd dug out the plates and cutlery, Piper was already busy building them sandwiches. The urge to take hold of her and kiss that soft mouth, stroke her all over, was so strong he had to curl his hands into fists to keep from reaching for her.

She had no clue how much he wanted to lay her out

on the blanket right now and settle on top of her just so he could finally feel her underneath him. Then kiss her until she was breathless and squirming, no more protests or excuses why they couldn't be together, then undress her and explore every inch of her body with his hands and mouth.

He shifted to relieve the sudden pressure of his erection shoved against his fly, but it didn't ease the ache in his cock.

"Here," she murmured, handing him a sandwich on a paper plate, along with some peach slices. All he could think about was feeding her the peaches and cream puffs, watching those plump pink lips close around each bite and then licking them clean himself.

Ignoring his body's demand to touch her, he accepted the sandwich and stretched out on his side, propping himself on one elbow while he ate.

"Oh, man, this tastes fantastic," she moaned around a bite of sandwich.

That sound didn't help the fit of his jeans any. To make matters worse, he knew she wanted him, no matter how hard she fought it, and he didn't know how much longer he could keep from talking about last night. "Sandwiches always taste better on picnics. Remember we used to take them down to the race track on Saturday nights?"

She hummed in agreement and continued eating. "Your dad would always pick up fried chicken and root beer on the way."

Those were good times. He had a thousand memories like that, of spending time with Piper and his family. She'd been part of his life—of his heart—for so long, he couldn't bear the thought of losing her.

After she finished her sandwich she turned her attention to the creek and watched the rippling water move past. He could tell from her expression that things were about to get serious. "So, about last night."

He stopped chewing, had to swallow hard to get the bite of sandwich down his suddenly tight throat. He didn't say anything, just waited for her to continue.

"What you said…surprised me. But you never said what you wanted to happen between us." She shot him a hesitant look, the set of her shoulders tense. "You know I'm leaving soon. So is it a short term thing for you, or…?"

What? "No," he answered, his voice so guttural it came out almost a growl. He didn't resent the question, given her need for caution and his past track record of flings, but hell, short term was the exact opposite of what he wanted.

Some of the wariness faded from her expression. "So you want…what then?" She picked up a peach slice and bit into it, and his gaze caught on her lips as her tongue flicked out to lick up the juice.

He imagined capturing her face between his hands and leaning in to lick it up himself before pushing between those gorgeous lips to finally taste her. The picture in his head damn near made him shudder.

He tore his gaze from her mouth and looked into her eyes. "I want you. Long term and definitely exclusive." Telling her he wanted to marry her and have a family together would definitely freak her out, so he withheld that.

For some reason, his answer seemed to surprise her, because her eyes widened slightly. "Oh."

The response gave him no clue what she was thinking and it drove him crazy. *What do you want?* He bit back the question even though it sat there burning on the end of his tongue.

Something in his expression must have tipped her off to his thoughts because she stilled in the act of biting into a piece of peach. Her hand fell to her lap, the half-finished slice still held between her fingers.

Easton held her gaze for a long moment, and as the silence stretched between them, something hot and electric crackled in the air. Her pupils expanded, and the way she watched him, tentative but with so much longing, made his whole body go hard. He couldn't look away, couldn't hide his response or his need for her a moment longer.

Sitting up, he slid the plate from her lap and the fruit from her fingers.

The gentle bubbling of the creek against the smooth stones at the bottom filled the charged silence as he maintained eye contact and slid his hands into her hair. A dare of sorts. Piper sucked in a soft breath and stayed absolutely still, gazing up at him.

Even though everything in him was dying to plunder that lush, sexy mouth, he knew it was too much too fast. Instead he swept his thumbs over her cheeks and leaned in to press a kiss to the center of her forehead.

She gasped but didn't pull away, so he followed the line of her nose from bridge to tip, paused there a moment before changing direction and kissing his way across her cheek, to her temple, and down the side of her jaw.

She set a hand on his left shoulder, her touch light, tentative, and her eyelashes fluttered as she closed her eyes. He almost groaned in relief at the tiny surrender and worked his way to the point of her chin, using his hands to tip her head back so he could trail more kisses up the other side of her jaw.

Her other hand came up to settle on his right shoulder, fingers flexing, squeezing, her breath uneven against his face.

Encouraged, Easton continued the slow exploration, caressing the tender spot below her ear for a moment, then he kissed the slope of her cheekbone and moved up to press a tender kiss to her eyelid.

Her fingers dug harder into his shoulders, her body swaying forward. He gathered her closer, hands stroking her hair, bunching it in his fingers as he kissed her other eyelid. An electric current seemed to sizzle between them, the very air alive with possibility.

Holding her head between his hands, he skimmed his lips down her cheek to the corner of her mouth and hovered there, waiting. Willing her to turn into him, to meet him partway.

Her head turned a fraction, her lips less than an inch from his while the blood pumped hot through Easton's body. He brushed a kiss over the edge of her mouth. Lighter than a sigh, a mere whisper of contact, his heart pounding out of control and every muscle drawn tight with desire.

Piper made a soft, helpless sound and closed the tiny gap between them, settling her mouth against his. A shockwave of sensation sliced through him, made him groan as he parted his lips to glide his tongue across the seam of her mouth.

Open for me, sweetness. Let me in. I'll be so good to you. He was dying to taste her, damn near shaking with it.

And she did open for him. Mother of Christ, she did, so slowly it made his hands tremble, that show of trust and need shaking him.

He delved inside for just a moment, allowing himself the briefest taste before withdrawing and sucking at her full lower lip. Her hands released his shoulders to creep up to his nape and squeeze as her tongue darted out to touch his.

Fire exploded in his gut. He barely managed to bite back a groan as he cradled the back of her head with one hand and slid the other down her back to pull her closer. The little purr she gave as she leaned into him and opened wider set his heart pounding.

He nudged his tongue against hers, caressed it. Piper let out a soft moan and gripped his nape harder, coming up on her knees to press the lushness of her breasts to his chest.

She tasted like peaches and smelled like heaven and he couldn't get enough of her. Again and again he tasted her, seducing her with gentle strokes of his tongue, a soft caress to the roof of her mouth while his heart thudded and his cock throbbed for more contact.

The energy between them shifted then and she grew bolder, more demanding, her fingers holding the sides of his face now as she licked and sucked at his mouth like she was starving for him. She whimpered and rubbed her breasts against his chest and his vow to take things slow vanished in a puff of smoke.

Without losing contact with her mouth he shifted and rolled them so that she was lying on her back. He came up on his elbows atop her, and when she wound her arms around his back to pull him closer, slowly lowered his weight into the cradle of her body. He groaned into her mouth at the feel of her body cushioning his for the first time, his head spinning and the need for relief a searing fire in his cock.

Careful not to crush her, he shifted his hips and settled his erection against her center.

Piper shuddered and rolled her hips, twining her legs with his to hold him close. He slowed the kiss and made love to her mouth, reveled in the tiny whimpers she made as he nibbled and sucked at her lips and slowly rocked the bulge in his jeans against her core. Christ, he'd imagined this so many times, and now that it was actually happening he almost felt drunk.

"Easton." Her raw whisper threatened to slice through the last threads of his control.

"I know," he whispered back, tipping her head back

to trail kisses across her jaw to her throat. He licked at the pulse beating so frantically beneath her tender skin, raked his teeth across it gently and felt the tiny shudder that ripped through her.

She shook her head and he kissed her again to stop whatever she was going to say. He didn't want her to think, didn't want her to question this or feel guilty about it. He only wanted her to feel, to give her all the pleasure he'd been dreaming about for so long.

It's too soon.

The stark whisper at the back of his mind cleared his head like a bucket of cold water to the face. She'd responded to him more perfectly than he could ever have wanted, but if he kept going things were going to get out of hand in a hurry.

There was no way he'd let her use her desire as an excuse to run from him. If he kept going, they'd both wind up naked and he'd be buried balls deep inside of her before he even realized what he'd done.

Charlie's earlier words came back to him, about Piper being hurt and wary. He didn't want to fuck up his only chance with her. She hadn't made any commitment to him and he refused to let this be just physical between them.

This wasn't a game. She wasn't some random woman he was looking to have a good time with. It was Piper, and he wanted all of her. So he had to slow things down, no matter how much it killed him.

He kissed her softly for another few heartbeats, then made himself raise his head. Her chest rose and fell with each rapid breath and he could feel the tension humming through her body.

With gentle sweeps of his hands over her face and hair, he soothed her as he nibbled his way across her mouth. Showing her without words how much he cherished her, proving he was willing to take things slow.

When he finally lifted his head a minute later, she stared up at him in confusion, her cheeks flushed with arousal. "Why did you stop?"

"Because I don't want to lose you by rushing this. And because I want all of you, not just your body."

She drew her fingertips down the side of his face, her eyes soft with understanding. And a regret that made his heart clench. "I don't know if I can give you what you want," she whispered, confirming that he'd made the right call in stopping.

Be patient with her. She wasn't ready yet to take the step he needed her to, so he had to back off.

"Yes you can, you're just scared to right now, and I understand that." Biting back a groan, he softened his words with a kiss, then rolled off her and got to his knees, grimacing as his erection pushed against his zipper. When his phone rang, it was almost a relief. He got up and grabbed it from his saddlebag. It was his teammate, Jamie.

His buddy had shitty timing. Or maybe great timing, depending on whatever Piper had been about to say to him. "Hey," he answered, part of him grateful for the reprieve. "You on your way down?"

"Nah, I'm already here, got in a few minutes ago. Your dad says you went out riding with someone."

Easton bit back a sigh. "Yeah." He guessed it wouldn't be cool of him to ask Jamie to hang out with his dad for a few hours while he and Piper talked this out, but he'd said all he had to say, and had to give her time to think now anyway, so leaving was for the best. "I'll head back now. Should be there in half an hour or so. You can meet me at the barn if you want. I've gotta untack the horses and brush them out."

"Okay, man, sounds good."

Slipping the phone into the front pocket of his flannel

shirt, Easton steeled himself and turned around to face Piper.

"Was that Brody?"

"No, a teammate I invited down to spend a couple days." And now he wondered what the fuck he'd been thinking when he had. Hanging with Jamie was the last damn thing on his mind now that he'd finally had a taste of Piper, but maybe it was good to give them a little break from each other.

"Oh." She looked uncertain as she crossed her arms over her breasts and cleared her throat. "We should get going then."

"Yeah." He took her hand in his, bent to press a kiss to her knuckles before pulling her to her feet.

Their interlude might be over but they still had unfinished business between them to settle. Before his time home came to an end on Sunday night, he intended to make her his.

Chapter TEN

Charlie stumbled down the stairs the next morning, eyes still half-closed. She didn't even know what time it was because she'd left her phone downstairs last night but the sun was already up so it had to be after seven.

After getting only a handful of hours of sleep she was in desperate need of coffee and had smelled it brewing from up in her room. She yawned and scratched at her shoulder as she hit the last step—and jerked to a halt when she saw the man standing in her childhood home's kitchen.

His back was to her but there was no mistaking who it was.

Agent Jamie Rodriguez. Tall, built, dark-haired, bronzed-skinned and sexy-beyond-all-reason man she'd gotten a taste of and wished she'd gotten a helluva lot more.

"What are you doing here?" she blurted, surprise obliterating her manners. It wasn't uncommon for one of them to invite someone to spend time at the farm, but Easton hadn't mentioned anything to her about this. He must have forgotten with everything that had been going on with Piper.

He turned to face her, his expression both wary and amused. "Easton invited me down to stay a few days if I wanted. Hello to you again too, by the way."

She ignored the last part. "Wait, you're *staying* here?" On her family's property? Where she'd have to see him on-and-off for the duration of his stay?

"Yeah, here." His lips twitched, his eyes daring her to say anything about it.

Well, damn. She looked away from his chiseled face to the coffee machine set on the counter, next to the sink. "Did you make that?"

"I did. Want some?"

Her gaze snapped back to him. Maybe he didn't mean it as an innuendo, but it sure sounded like one and the heated, lazy look in his eyes made heat flare inside her. "Yeah," she fired back.

He stilled, surprise lighting the depths of those amber-brown eyes for a moment as her meaning registered. Without a word he turned away to get a mug down from the cupboard and then filled it, allowing her to look her fill at the way he filled out his T-shirt and jeans. The man was ripped.

Her socked-feet were silent on the wooden floorboards as she crossed the room to take the mug he handed her. "Thanks." He was even bigger up close, about the size of Wyatt. She wasn't a tiny woman but standing next to him she felt like she was, and he made all her senses buzz with female awareness.

"Welcome. I already got the sugar and cream out."

"I like my coffee dark, and I don't take sugar because I'm sweet enough as it is."

One side of his mouth lifted. "Are you?"

"Well, apparently my mouth is. You don't remember?" she asked, feigning insult.

You taste so damn sweet.

As his words from a few months ago echoed in the silence between them, his smile disappeared. "I remember," he murmured, and stepped away to put the creamer back in the fridge. Trying to escape her? Interesting.

She'd met him at a club back in April, where she'd gone with a few co-workers. He'd been there with some other DEA people and the spark between them had been instant and undeniable.

A few hours of dancing and flirting had led to the single hottest make-out session she'd ever experienced while clothed, up against the wall outside the back of the club. And then he'd found out her last name and disappeared. No calls, no texts. Nothing.

It hadn't been until she'd done some digging a few days later that she'd found out why. He was her brother's teammate.

"So, you guys just got back from A-stan the other day, huh?"

He nodded. "When did you get here?"

"Couple nights ago." She tossed her hair over her shoulder. "You staying in the cabin with Easton?"

"Yes. I parked out behind the barn. We're out of coffee over there so I had to come in here."

That explained why she hadn't seen his truck when she'd gotten home at two this morning. And at least it meant she wouldn't have to be tortured with his presence in the house often.

"Where were you last night?" he asked, sounding curious.

"Out with friends." She sipped her coffee and went over to sit at the table, turning her chair to face him. "So. How do you want to do this?"

He blinked. "What do you mean?"

"Are we going to tell Easton we've met before, or do you want to pretend we just met now?"

"We'll tell him we met before."

But we won't tell him that you had your hands and mouth all over me outside that club. She nodded once. "Okay."

She liked him, wanted the chance to get to know him better, but it wasn't like she wanted anything long term. People thought Easton was the wild one in the family, but she was wild too—just in a more subtle way. She was only twenty-eight, and not in any hurry to settle down.

Charlie didn't see the point in not going after what she wanted. After losing her mom at a young age, then nearly losing both her dad and Wyatt within the space of a year, she knew exactly how short life was.

"Did Easton tell you what's been going on here?" she asked.

"Sort of. He said that there's a situation going down with someone close to you guys."

"Piper. She's like family to us." And, if she read Easton right, maybe one day Piper would actually become a Colebrook.

She gave a quick rundown of what had happened, leaving out the part about Easton's feelings for Piper. "If you had plans to fish and ride and hunt, you might have to do all that solo this visit, because Easton's going to be sticking close to her."

Hopefully *really* close. She wanted her brother to be happy, and thought he and Piper were a good match. But this had just as much chance of ending in heartbreak as it did in a happily-ever-after, and that was what worried her most.

"Okay, good to know."

She raised an eyebrow. "If I get some time later,

maybe I'll take you out…riding."

He paused with his mug partway to his mouth, his dark-honey stare locked on hers. Slowly, he lowered his mug. "Yeah?"

She shrugged, enjoying the flirtatious banter. It had been way too long since any man had fired her up, and this one had practically incinerated her with his kisses. "Maybe. Depends on how you play your cards."

He tilted his head a fraction, and she loved that he didn't back down from the subtle gauntlet she'd thrown down. "I think you'd find I'm pretty good at it. I love to ride, as long as I'm the one holding the reins."

His sexy challenge sent an invisible shiver through her and her heart rate quickened. There was no mistaking what he meant, and it confirmed what she'd sensed in him that night in April. He liked control, and that meant in the bedroom as well. Imagining the many ways that would translate into sex with him made her mouth go dry.

"I'll bear that in mind," she murmured, managing to keep her voice steady.

"You do that, *pequeña*."

Little one.

Her abdomen fluttered at his deep, intimate tone. As she sat there staring at him while desire rushed through her body, without another word he set his mug in the sink and walked past her, out the back door.

As his footsteps receded in the distance, Charlie smiled to herself and leaned back in her chair. Well, well. It appeared things weren't finished between them after all.

****

"Is this smooth enough now?" Piper leaned back to squint at the spot on the wall she'd just sanded for what felt like the eighth time.

Easton paused rolling paint on the opposite wall to set down the roller and come hunker down next to her. He ran a hand over the spot, the muscles in his arm flexing, and her nipples tightened, her breasts growing heavy at the thought of feeling that hand on her naked skin later.

After the picnic yesterday and that mind-blowing make-out session, getting naked with him was all she'd been able to think about, no matter how hard she'd tried to stop. She still couldn't believe she'd given into temptation like that. Now the desire was worse than ever.

"Yeah, looks good. Give it a wipe and I'll start on the wall as soon as I'm done with this one. Shouldn't take me more than fifteen minutes to do both." His knees cracked as he pushed to his feet and returned to his paint tray.

The kisses they'd shared had been wonderful, but they hadn't changed her mind about moving. She was taking that job waiting for her.

It was still so hard to believe that Easton wanted her, let alone how much. She'd never known her body could come alive like that. Then he'd touched her, kissed her, blanketed her with his body and made her liquid with need. He'd answered her questions yesterday and told her what he wanted, but she still sensed he was holding something back. Something important.

She was dying to know what it was, and a little afraid, too.

There were so many things she admired about him. His loyalty, his work ethic. She loved that he was dependable and protective. And holy hell, the man was sexy. He tied her in knots without even trying, and yesterday…

Leaving him behind when she moved was going to be

hard, but he was leaving for Alexandria and then back overseas again soon anyway. She'd never imagined what it would feel like to be the center of attention for a man with his kind of sensuality. It was so natural from him, simply a part of who he was. Every time she looked at him now her heart thudded. And when he looked at her…

She blew out a breath and took out her dusting rag to wipe down the wall and floor to get rid of the sanding dust. Her mind wouldn't let the idea of them together go. Was he really able to commit to her that seriously?

She was lonely, true, but also bitterly disappointed by her marriage and afraid to risk opening her heart to a man again. While she didn't think Easton would ever hurt her the way Greg had if they got involved, the idea still scared her to death. If Easton hurt her it would be worse than with Greg because he wasn't selfish and wouldn't do it on purpose.

Sex with Easton would be powerful and raw, but once the initial fireworks and excitement wore off, would he lose interest? He'd built her up in his head for so many years. He'd have certain expectations. What if the reality of being with her didn't measure up? She didn't want to find out she was a disappointment.

She was on her way to the kitchen to check if Charlie needed help when her phone rang. It was the lead detective on her case. "Hello."

"Hi. We've got a possible lead I want to talk to you about. Can you come down to the station?"

She glanced over at Easton, who'd stopped and was watching her, his roller still on the wall. "Sure. Give me twenty minutes."

"Is Agent Colebrook there with you?"

"Yes, he is."

"Bring him too."

"Okay." She'd planned to anyway.

Easton drove her to the station and sat next to her while the detective and FBI agent laid out what the latest developments were. They hadn't found a print on the tracking device, and techs were still trying to trace the signal back to whoever had been monitoring it.

"We've done some digging, and managed to come up with a possible suspect," the detective said, turning the computer screen on the desk to face them. A man's mug shot appeared, along with his name. Brandon Gallant.

Easton tensed and sat forward, his attention riveted to the screen. Piper glanced at him.

"You recognize him?" the detective asked him.

"Yeah." Easton sat back and rubbed a hand over his mouth. "We did a raid a few years back in D.C. and arrested him. Drug trafficker."

The FBI agent nodded and folded his arms across his chest. "That's right. Our records indicate that Mr. Rutland had dealings with Gallant while he was sheriff." His gaze shifted to Piper. "Is he familiar to you at all?"

She shook her head. "No, not at all, and I don't recognize the name either."

"Given the history between him and your ex-husband, and the connection with Agent Colebrook, we feel it's best that you take precautions until Gallant is apprehended."

"She's staying at my family's property outside of town," Easton said. "One of my teammates is there as well. She'll be well protected."

The agent nodded. "Good."

Outside in the hallway, Piper grasped Easton's forearm and he stopped and looked at her. "Maybe I should leave town for a while. Until they catch him."

Easton's mouth thinned into a flat line and he shook his head. "You're safe with us. My family is trained, and no one's as motivated to keep you safe as we are. I won't entrust your safety to strangers, Piper, so don't ask me to."

She blinked at him, taken aback by his vehemence. His family had been through more than enough already without taking on more of her shit.

He sighed and softened his expression. "Look, all of us know that land like the backs of our hands. You've got Jamie and me there, and Charlie can handle herself, and my dad can still shoot just fine with his left hand. If anyone comes looking for you there, they'll be sorry. And if necessary, we can use one of the trails to get you out of there."

Chapter ELEVEN

Hands in the pockets of his leather jacket, Brandon stayed in the shadows and watched as two of his men supervised Greg while he searched through the storage unit. They'd had to wait until the security shift change at two in the morning. A few hundred bucks in product for the new guard, and he'd been happy to go on break to get his fix and let them do whatever they wanted.

"Make sure you check everything in there," he said, watching with a sharp eye.

Before he'd been a corrupt sheriff, Greg had served in the Army and done combat tours. He was better trained than Brandon and his hired muscle. Even beaten to a pulp and half-starved, Greg was a threat. If he made a move to try and escape, Brandon would shoot him dead before he ever made it out of the storage unit.

"We got nothing, boss," one of his men said a few minutes later.

"Because it's not here," Greg said, his voice strained

and angry. "Like I already told you, it's not goddamn *here*."

"So where is it then?" Brandon demanded. He'd had to bring his own men here to check things out, to make sure Greg wasn't lying. Because he was one of the best liars around.

"I don't know." Greg hunched over and winced, put a hand to his ribs. "I've already looked everywhere."

This whole protective thing he had going on for his ex-wife was working to Brandon's advantage. "Then we'll get Piper and make her show us."

In the bright beam of the flashlight one of his men had aimed at him, Greg paled. "No. There's one more place we can check without involving her."

"Where?"

"She said she'd stored some stuff at a friend's place."

"Who?"

He hesitated a moment before answering. "The Colebrook place."

No way. Brandon bit back a laugh. This was too good. Might be the perfect opportunity to get everything he wanted. "She's staying there with him. Easton."

Greg's eyes snapped to his, disbelief and pain clouding them.

"For a few days now, at least." Brandon let that verbal blade sink deep. "You didn't know?"

"They're friends," he said in a defensive tone.

"Oh, they're more than friends. I've got pictures to prove it. Wanna see them?"

Greg looked away, jaw flexing. "No."

Brandon would make sure to show him when they got back to the house and locked Greg back up in his prison. The son of a bitch deserved some psychological torture after the way he'd betrayed him.

"I've had the place scoped out and my men have been watching her closely, following her movements." Up until someone had discovered the tracking device, anyway. He was betting Easton. “So far there hasn’t been an opportunity to take her because she’s never alone. Easton’s taking advantage of the opportunity because he’s keeping her close to him. *Real* close, according to what I’ve seen.”

Greg’s nostrils flared. He glared at Brandon, unmoving.

“That property they’ve got out there is something else,” he continued. “Nice old house, matching cabin. Apparently over a hundred-and-fifty-years old. Probably worth a lot. Shame to see it all destroyed because you can’t return what you stole from me.”

Greg’s gaze snapped back to his, the blue eyes bright as lasers. “If you’re thinking about attacking the Colebrooks, you’re fucking insane.”

He smiled slowly. “Am I?” It would send a message. Hurting Piper would hurt Greg. And killing Easton would satisfy Brandon immensely.

“Easton is DEA. Another brother is with the FBI’s Hostage Rescue Team, and the oldest is a Marine combat vet.”

“With a prosthetic leg and artificial eye, yeah, I heard.”

“Both his gun hands still work just fine.”

“He isn’t even living there anymore. He’s shacked up with his girlfriend in town. By the time word got out about the attack, it would be too late for him to get there.”

“The sister is DEA too. She and the old man might not be as much of a threat as the others, but they’re still deadly shots and if you attack, they’ll shoot to kill.”

Brandon’s expression hardened. “I don’t fucking care. I don’t care who they are or how fucking many of them are there or not. I want my shit back, and I want it *now*.”

If he couldn't get his goods back the easy way, then he'd do it the messy way. The time was coming where he'd have to get reckless and stage an attack on the property no matter the threat the Colebrooks posed. There was no way to get into the house without a direct assault and risk attack from the family.

"Let me see if I can find the cabinet there first," Greg said.

Brandon pulled his hands from his pockets and folded his arms across his chest. "I'm listening."

"The outbuildings are easier to search, but it's gonna be tricky because of the constant movement of people around there. Farmhands and other workers, as well as the family. It'll have to be in the middle of the night, and it'll have to be totally covert."

He snorted. "If you mean you want to go in alone, think again, asshole."

"I'm trained. Better trained than they are," Greg said, disdain dripping from his voice as he jerked his chin at the two men Gallant had brought with them. "If they screw up and alert anyone that we're there, the Colebrooks will shoot first and ask questions later. They know I'm missing, and after you trashed Piper's place they'll think she's in danger too. They'll be on alert. That's why she's staying there. For protection."

"Whatever you need to tell yourself to help you sleep better," Brandon mocked. "But I'm not worried. It's not my neck on the line, it's yours. And Piper's," he added, letting the threat hit home. "Either you deliver, or she dies. It's as simple as that."

Greg fell silent, his hate-filled stare burning through Brandon.

I hate you more, you piece of shit. He turned away, walked off into the darkness. "Burn it," he ordered his men, and headed for the car while they doused the storage unit with gasoline. It was time to make a move.

****

When the bedroom door down the hall opened in the middle of the night, Easton opened his eyes and stared up at the darkened ceiling of the cabin's living room where he was bunking on the couch. He'd put Jamie in the house and moved Piper in here with him so he could watch out for her personally, but also because he wanted privacy with her.

He hadn't touched her intimately or tried to kiss her again since the picnic, and she'd been carefully keeping her distance from him too.

It was driving him nuts, but at least he wasn't the only one suffering because apparently Piper couldn't sleep either.

He sat up and pulled on his jeans before stepping out into the hallway. "Hey. You okay?"

She stopped and turned to face him, her curvy silhouette outlined by the weak moonlight filtering in through the windows in the kitchen. She had on stretchy black pants that hugged every curve of her lower body, and a baggy sweater that came to the top of her hips.

He wanted to mold his hands to the curve of her ass, squeeze it and then slide them up beneath that loose sweater to feel the smooth skin of her back beneath his palms.

"Yeah. Just can't sleep. Did I wake you?"

"No." He couldn't sleep when he was tormented by the memory of how she'd felt and tasted today. He wanted her so badly it tied him in knots to stay in his own bed when he'd rather be in hers. Even just so he could hold her in the darkness.

"I was going to sit out on the porch swing for a bit." She tucked her hair behind her ear. "Want to join me?"

At this point he'd take any excuse to spend time

alone with her and erase the distance between them. “Sure.”

She stopped in the kitchen to pour herself a glass of water then walked through the living room and out into the screen porch where the swing sat off to one end. He’d swept the front of the property and secured the cabin earlier before turning in, so he felt okay with letting her sit out here.

Easton lowered himself next to her onto the wide, deep seat and grabbed a throw blanket from a basket on the floor. The nights were already crisp and cool and a chilly breeze blew through the screens.

He shook it out and draped the folds over them both. She gave him a soft smile of thanks and tucked her feet under her, cuddling up beneath the blanket. He’d rather she cuddled up beneath him instead.

Crickets and frogs sang in the background, mixing with the gentle breeze that carried the scent of damp grass. “I feel so guilty, sitting here all safe and warm while he’s either being held hostage or worse. Even though he brought it on himself, I hate knowing he’s going through that.”

Piper had a huge heart. It was what Easton loved most about her, and why he hated Greg’s guts for stomping all over it. “I understand.”

Needing to at least touch her, he draped his arm across her shoulders and let his fingers play with the ends of her soft hair. He couldn’t believe how nervous he was, sitting next to her like this in the moonlight.

For months he’d devised a plan to make her his, but now he felt like he was treading on eggshells. One wrong move and he’d ruin everything. His heart thudded in his chest, about to burst with his feelings for her.

Piper stared down at the folds of the blanket rather than look at him. “What you said before, about us.” Her gaze lifted to his. “When you said long term, what did you mean, exactly?"

He raised an eyebrow. "Are you sure you want to know the answer to that?"

"Yes."

"I want it all."

She stared at him in silence, a frown puckering her brow.

She wanted him to spell it out? He hated putting himself out there like this and making himself totally vulnerable when he didn't know what her response would be, but he couldn't hold back anymore. So he just said it. "I love you. I've loved you forever."

She went dead still and stared at him with shocked hazel eyes. "You love me?"

"I'm *in* love with you." There was a big difference.

She looked away, didn't respond for a long moment and a lick of panic flared inside him. "I…I didn't know."

No, because he'd held it back for fear of scaring her away. If he thought for one second that she didn't want him the same way he wanted her, he'd drop it.

But she did.

Maybe she wasn't ready to admit the full extent of her feelings for him, but she wanted him, physically at least, and she loved him at least a little, he was sure of it.

She looked over at him again. "All these years, you never did or said anything to let me know."

"You were married."

"You came to the wedding."

"Hated every second of it, but yeah."

"Why? Why would you come and watch me marry another man if you loved me?"

Because I'm a masochist. "Because I didn't want to let you down."

Her eyes filled with sadness, regret. "I'm sorry, that must have been awful. I never meant to hurt you."

"I know. But I freely admit that was the second-worst

day of my life, after my mom died." And a few years after Piper had married that asshole, Wyatt was wounded and their dad had the stroke.

A sad smile quirked her mouth. "You hid it well. You came up and hugged me and kissed my cheek after the ceremony." She swallowed. "Then you wished me the best and told me to be happy."

He nodded. He'd been dying inside, knowing she legally belonged to another man, thinking he'd lost her forever. "I've always wanted you to be happy. Even if it wasn't with me."

"But I wasn't." She studied him with haunted eyes. "And you knew I wouldn't be, didn't you?"

"It doesn't matter what I thought."

She shook her head, her eyes shimmering with tears and the sight gutted him. He curved a hand around the side of her face, rubbed his thumb over the silky softness of her cheek. "Don't cry," he whispered, aching.

"Why didn't you say anything?" She wiped impatiently at her eyes.

"Would you have left him if I had?"

"No, and I wouldn't have believed you back then anyway," she admitted, sounding miserable as she lowered her gaze and drew in a shaky breath. She didn't pull away from him though. "God, I was so stupid."

Easton didn't blame her for saying she wouldn't have believed him back then. He'd been hell on wheels when he'd come out of the Marine Corps. Fast women, faster cars. Since joining the DEA he'd grown up a lot, matured so much since then. "He fooled a lot of people for a long time. Even his own parents."

She was quiet a moment. "I knew he had problems. He dazzled me, I guess is the right way to describe it. Swept me off my feet and I thought when he hit a rocky patch that things would get better, because we loved each other. That he would be able to cut back on the drinking and the meds. I had reservations going in, I saw the signs, and yet I ignored that little voice in the back of my head that told me not to go through with it. I made a huge mistake, and I'm still paying for it." Raising her head, she met his eyes and the haunted look in them made his heart squeeze. "I didn't see the truth until it was too late."

Was she talking about him as well? His pulse beat faster, hope and anticipation ballooning inside him. "Me neither. I didn't know how bad things had gotten until I was home last time. I hate that you went through all that."

"It doesn't matter now." She shook her head, her expression full of amazement. "All this time, I never saw you."

He didn't say anything, just held her gaze and waited as a long, loaded silence pressed between them. *I'm right here in front of you now. I've been here all along.*

Slowly she turned her body toward him, pulled an arm from beneath the blanket and reached up to cup the side of his face. "But I see you now," she murmured. "I can't *not* see you, no matter how hard I try. And I don't know what the hell to do about that."

Every muscle in his body tightened. He felt that innocent touch everywhere, and her words exploded through him in a heated rush that made him dizzy. There was no time now for the romantic, seductive plan he'd envisioned for them these past few months. Not with her still set on leaving and the threat to her safety hanging over their heads.

"Maybe you should just trust your heart then, and let go of everything else."

She gave a rueful snort and shook her head. "I don't trust my heart anymore."

"Yes you do. You're just afraid to follow it."

"Yeah, I'm terrified. I don't want to mess up what we

have."

He leaned closer, unwilling to let this go. Not when he was so close to winning her. "I won't hurt you. I'm not him."

"I know. But I'm afraid of losing you if we go through with this."

"You won't lose me. Not ever."

"It could wreck our friendship if things don't work out. It could wreck my relationship with your entire family."

"We're adults, Piper. All of us. We'd figure it out."

She blew out a breath, looking tortured and completely unconvinced. "What if I can't give you what you're asking for?" she said, repeating almost the same words from down by the creek.

"What if you can?"

She closed her eyes, shook her head. So afraid to follow her instincts and take what she wanted. What they both needed.

He skimmed his fingertips along her jaw, savoring the softness of her skin. "We both know it'll be good."

Her eyes opened, the pupils dilating in the dimness. They dropped to his mouth for a second before coming back to his and the desire and longing burning in them made his gut clench. "But does that make it worth the risk?"

He'd prove to her that it was. "Only one way to find out." He bent his head and covered her lips with his, her swift intake of breath setting a match to the desire roaring through him. He slid a hand into her hair, his fingers bunching in the cool, silky strands as he pushed his tongue into her mouth.

Instead of pushing him away, Piper scooted up on her knees and gripped his head as she kissed him back, rubbing her tongue against his, her breasts pressed to his chest. The taste of her, the sweet scent of her perfume and the pliant curves of her body surrounded him in a sensual fog.

Giving into temptation for just a moment, he slid his right arm down until his hand met the curve of her ass. He spread his fingers, squeezed as he brought her pelvis flush with his thigh. She gasped into his mouth and shifted her stance, pressing closer. Close enough so that he could feel her heat through his jeans as he twined his tongue with hers.

Yellow light. Slow down.

Much as it killed him to stop and let her go, he had to. She wanted him, at least believed that he loved her, and that was a good start, but she was still fighting the rest of it and he didn't know what the hell else to do except give her the space to make the choice herself.

If and when she came to him, it would be because she couldn't stay away any longer. She had to give him her heart freely and on her own, not because of pressure, or it would never last.

And with Piper, he was playing for keeps. All or nothing, simple as that.

Gently disengaging from the kiss, he gazed into her heavy-lidded eyes a moment, then stood and offered his hand. "Come lie down with me so I can hold you."

She stilled and watched him, all her emotions right there in her eyes. Hesitation, doubt. A need he was dying to satisfy but wouldn't, not unless she gave him all of her.

He waited, unmoving, holding her gaze until the tension bled out of her shoulders. At last she put her hand in his, allowed him to pull her to her feet. Maybe things hadn't gone according to his grand romantic plan, but he could still sweep her off her feet better than Greg had.

Sliding one arm around her back, he bent and tucked the other one beneath her knees, swinging her up into his arms. She let out a little squeak and then laughed, the happy sound flowing through him as she looped both arms around his neck and held on. “Don’t drop me.”

He stopped and looked down into her eyes. “I’d never let you fall.”

A slow, poignant smile curved her lips and he couldn’t resist tasting her. He kissed her slowly, heart thudding at the way she turned her face up to him, her mouth parting for the lazy stroke of his tongue.

Leaving her wanting more, he smiled to himself as he carried her through the door into the living room, through the kitchen and down the hall to his room. The covers were already turned back so he laid her down then crawled over her and lay on his side. He wrapped one arm around her ribs to pull her in tight to his body.

He was rock hard and aching but she didn’t wriggle away, and though he wanted nothing more than to strip her naked and slide into her warmth, he loved the feel of her settled against him like this. Soft and trusting.

He’d waited more than a decade for her, and now he was finally on the verge of winning her. No matter how hard it was, he had to be patient and let her come to him. It was the only way to claim her heart as well as her body.

Chapter TWELVE

It really does rain when it pours.

Piper sat next to Easton at the lead detective's desk down at the police station the next morning and suppressed a tired sigh. She'd woken in Easton's arms with a call saying that her storage unit had been torched sometime last night, so she'd had to come down here again.

"I'm sorry to say that everything in the unit was a total loss," the detective said.

Piper's heart sank when he slid an open folder across the desk to her and she saw what was left of her things. Nothing but blackened, charred piles of rubble where the bulk of her belongings had once been.

"They closed the door after setting the fire, and the metal insulated everything, making the fire hotter than normal. Three other units were destroyed as well before the fire crews were able to put it out."

Most of her clothes, her books, her furniture and photo albums, including the pictures of her and her father. All gone. She swallowed the lump in her throat and pushed aside the sadness, telling herself it was just stuff, even though her heart didn't believe it. "Is there any video evidence?"

The detective shook his head. "Whoever set it disabled the cameras at the entrance to the facility and the ones near your unit. It was well-planned. They bribed the security guard on site and broke into your unit, then set it on fire before they left."

"Maybe they found whatever they were looking for."

"Maybe," he allowed, but his tone was doubtful.

"Was the guard charged?"

"Yes, and he's been fired. After he confessed, he gave details about who bribed him. Description matched Gallant."

"Any more word about Greg?"

"No, but we're almost certain Brandon Gallant is behind this. He's dangerous because he's unpredictable. He just got out of prison, and he's looking to make a name for himself. He has everything to gain by escalating the situation and using Greg's life as leverage."

Piper nodded. "I just want him found alive."

"We'll find him. Did you have a chance to go through the rest of your belongings in storage before last night?"

"Yes, Easton and I checked everything in the unit two nights ago, as well as the things in the shed at his family's place. We didn't find anything."

"And still no idea what it is Greg might have hidden? If we knew, we'd have a better sense of what we're up against."

She shook her head. "I have no idea. He did a lot of bad things, but he never involved me directly in any of it. He didn't tell me what he'd done because he didn't want me to know what he'd been up to, and he didn't want me implicated if it ever came to light. I think it was his backward way of protecting me." She shrugged. "It could be anything."

"They'll find him," Easton murmured, squeezing her hand.

She squeezed back, grateful for his solid, calming presence. This whole thing had exhausted her mentally and emotionally, but at least having Easton at her side made it a little easier to bear.

****

Hours later, she pressed a hand to her belly and took a slow, deep breath to quell the nerves buzzing there. All day long she'd thought about Easton and what tonight might bring.

Sleeping in his arms last night had cemented her decision about them. He'd done nothing but hold her, hadn't even kissed her or touched her except to stroke her hair and her back. He probably didn't realize it, but that simple act of intimacy had knocked down most of the wall she'd built around her heart.

She was still set on leaving for Minnesota, that part wasn't going to change. She would never risk their relationship or her bond with his family over a fling, and he'd made it clear he wanted all or nothing.

And yet, she'd never forgive herself for walking away without giving them a shot. So she'd decided to see what happened if she did.

Taking this next step with him terrified her, but it was also the most exciting thing she'd had to look forward to in her entire life. She trusted him.

If she was honest with herself, she'd fantasized about him for months and she was done with feeling guilty about it. They were both adults, they cared about and respected each other, and there was nothing stopping them from getting together right now except her fears.

Her vivid, deep-seated fears and insecurity.

She pushed the thought aside. “Okay, I think we’re finally done here.” She wiped the back of her sleeve across her damp forehead and wrung out the mop in the bucket then paused to survey their work.

She and Easton had been here for the past four hours, giving everything a thorough deep clean while Wyatt and Austen worked out in her yard, mowing the lawn and tidying the garden beds. Tomorrow she would go through her things stored in the shed at the Colebrook’s and take inventory of what she had left.

For now, everything here was clean and re-staged, ready for showings she would start booking tomorrow.

“Good, because I’m starving,” Easton murmured, walking up to set a hand on her waist and draw her into his body for a slow, melting kiss that made her knees go weak. His clean, masculine scent drowned out the smell of vinegar and lemon that hung heavy in the air.

She nipped playfully at his lower lip, his short beard prickling her softly. “Me too, but I want a shower first, because I’m all sweaty.”

“I think you taste amazing all sweaty.” He raised his head, his eyes going heavy-lidded as he gazed down at her. “How about we eat first, then shower together after.”

She laughed. “I want the first time you see me naked to be slightly more memorable than me standing in the shower looking like a drowned rat.”

He stilled and leaned back a little to study her, his eyes alight with interest and understanding. “I’m gonna get to see you naked?”

“Maybe. If you play your cards right. But not until after I’m clean.”

“The idea of you naked and wet works really well for me. You got something else in mind?”

"You'll have to see." If her nerve held up.

The back door opened and Wyatt's voice called out. "We're done out here. You guys ready yet?"

"Yeah, we were just saying how hungry we are," Easton said, holding her gaze. The heat smoldering there set off tingles inside her.

"Great, we'll grab something to eat before you guys head back to the house."

Easton raised an eyebrow at her in question. She shrugged and nodded. "Okay," Easton called back. "Be out in a minute."

He helped her put the cleaning supplies away then put her in his truck and it struck her again how even with everything that was happening, she felt totally safe here with him.

On the drive back to the house she reached for his hand and twined his fingers through hers. Easton was solid and protective, funny and sweet. He still had a bit of a wild streak and would probably always be an adrenaline junkie, but there was no way she was going to deny them both what they so desperately wanted.

They needed to be together tonight, and for as long as they had left, however long that may be.

Austen and Wyatt stopped on the way to the house to pick up pizza. Piper's nerves dissipated quickly and by the time they arrived with the food, she was enjoying herself. She even laughed a few times at stories Easton told. It felt so damn good.

After dinner she showered while Easton took one in the house. Standing under the hot spray as she shampooed her hair, however, the nerves hit her all over again. Every doubt she'd ever had about crossing the line with him bombarded her and she fought them off one at a time. Her mind was made up. She was doing this.

She took extra time getting ready, blow-dried her

hair, put on a little makeup and perfume before slipping into the one piece of lingerie she'd had at her house—a pale aqua satin slip trimmed with lace that came to her upper thighs.

Staring at herself in the mirror as she smoothed her hands down the sides of the cool, slippery satin, she balked. Every single insecurity about her body came back to hit her full force.

She was almost thirty-six and…rounded and soft instead of firm and taut. Nothing like the thin, fit women she'd seen Easton date in the past. Laugh lines etched the corners of her eyes and the crease in her cheek that had once resembled a dimple was now a definite wrinkle. Could he really want her when in the past he'd dated women who were her physical opposite?

Her heart pounded as she stood there looking at her reflection. If she walked out of here dressed like this, there was no turning back. Sleeping with him would change everything, and maybe not for the better. She refused to give him promises she didn't intend to keep.

"Piper? You okay in there?" he called through the door.

She closed her eyes. "Yes." *Just getting cold feet.*

"All right." His footsteps faded away toward the kitchen.

The momentary reprieve allowed her another minute to gather her courage. She tried for logic. They wanted each other and the attraction wasn't going away. They'd also known each other for damn near twenty years.

No, wait. Don't think about that. She cringed as a picture of thirteen-year-old Easton popped into her head. "Not helping," she muttered. "Not helping at all."

Okay. She forced herself to meet her gaze in the mirror. *You're a grown woman and you know what you want. So take it.*

Yeah, that was better. This was Easton. She'd known

him forever. He would be good to her, and he would never hurt her. At least not the way Greg had.

But what if this ruins everything? She narrowed her eyes at her reflection. "And what if it doesn't?" she countered, repeating Easton's words to her yesterday.

Her heart beat faster as she thought of him out there, waiting. He had to know what would happen when she stepped out of the bathroom. Heat bloomed in her belly and her breasts grew heavy, the nipples tightening beneath the satin.

She'd lived her whole life trying to play it safe, to always maintain control, and look where it had gotten her. She wasn't the same person as she'd been when she'd married Greg. Dammit, she deserved to be happy and have her needs met by a man who loved her.

Her courage rose and she focused on that thought, and on the man waiting for her outside this door. She was done holding back and letting fear and insecurity rule her life. Easton was out there and she was going after him. She wasn't sure what would happen between them after tonight but she didn't care—she needed him too much to turn down this chance.

Before she could talk herself out of it, she opened the door and stepped out into the hallway. Blood roared in her ears as a wave of cool air washed over her skin, hardening her nipples even more. A soft glow lit the darkness, coming from the living room. She followed it, her heart pounding.

When she reached the entryway to the living room, she stopped. Easton had lit a candle in the lantern on the center of the coffee table, giving the room a warm, romantic feel. A tremulous smile curved her lips as she watched him blow out the match he held.

He caught sight of her and turned, his eyes widening as he took in the pretty slip she wore. "Whoa," he breathed, his eyes never leaving her. Heat licked over her skin as he raked his gaze down the length of her body from head to toe and back.

She fought the urge to wrap her arms around herself, tried to disregard the terrible vulnerability of standing there before him like this, bare toes curling against the floorboards.

Then he advanced a step toward her, still staring at her with that hot, sexual gaze, and she began to fidget with the hem of the slip. His expression softened as he came to her. She swallowed, forced herself to move forward instead of backing away.

Erasing the remaining distance between them with a few strides, he stopped before her to curve his hands around her upper arms. "You're so gorgeous."

She could barely breathe and her heart was pounding so hard she was sure he must be able to hear it. "Thanks," she whispered.

He tilted his head, a disarming grin curving his lips. "Hey. You're not nervous, are you?"

A wheezy laugh escaped her. "I'm *so* nervous."

His warm brown eyes searched hers, a caress that resonated deep inside her. "With me?"

"Especially with you." No one had ever mattered to her the way he did. Not even Greg, and the admission made her wince inside. "I haven't done this in a long time, and I've wanted you for months now—"

"Wait," he said, clearly shocked. "Months?"

She nodded. "Since the last day I saw you. Maybe a little before, I don't know exactly when I started to see you differently."

Tenderness filled his gaze and he groaned softly. "I'm so damn glad you did," he said, then kissed her.

Need and desire sizzled through her veins. His hands came up to frame her face as he deepened the kiss, and the stroke of his tongue against hers set something free inside her. More. She needed more.

She slid her fingers into his hair and pressed against the lean, hard length of him, igniting a throb between her thighs. She reveled in the taste of him, his strength as he wrapped his arms around her back and pulled her close.

A shudder wracked her and her skin felt too tight, over sensitized. This man had turned her entire universe on its head, and being off-balance had never felt so good.

Craving the feel of his bare skin, she skimmed her hands down to slide them under the hem of his shirt. He released her long enough to reach back and grab a fistful of his shirt, then dragged it over his head and dropped it.

Piper stared, her mouth going dry as her heart thudded in her ears. The candlelight gilded every plane and hollow of his torso, highlighting the swells of the defined muscles of his chest, arms and stomach. So strong, but he always used that strength to protect and defend, had always been there for her. How had she not seen that before?

She flattened her hands on his pectorals, traced the powerful curves with her palms, need stirring low in her gut at his indrawn breath and the way his nipples tightened beneath her touch. She stroked and petted, memorizing the feel of him as she let her lips follow in the wake of her hands, her tongue flicking out to taste his hot skin.

“Bedroom,” he rasped out, keeping a firm hold on her as he walked her backward a few steps, then grabbed her bottom and hauled her into the air. She squeaked and wrapped her legs around him, bringing her mound against the hard length of his erection.

“You smell so damn good,” he growled, nipping at her lower lip as he carried her through the darkened kitchen and down the hall to the bedroom. Soft moonlight shone through the window beside the king-size bed, allowing her to see the hunger on his face.

He leaned over the bed and lowered her onto the covers but she refused to let him go, pulling him down on top of her. A plaintive moan slipped free at the feel of his hard weight pressing her down into the mattress, the thin chemise riding up to her hips. His body was the only thing anchoring her while the rest of the world spun and her heart pounded.

"I've thought about this so many times," she whispered.

"Mmm, me too." Easton kissed her jaw and laved his tongue against the side of her throat, his beard prickling gently as his hands cupped her breasts through the satin. She arched and released his head to tug the straps down over her shoulders, impatient for him to ease the ache in her breasts and between her legs.

A low groan eased from his chest as her breasts were revealed, her nipples tightening under the heat in his gaze. His big hands cupped them, his thumbs brushing over the centers, making her squirm and grab the back of his neck to drag him closer. He obliged, balancing his weight on one arm to lean down and take one into his mouth.

Heat flooded her. She gasped and pushed against his mouth, couldn't hold back a soft cry as he sucked and swirled his tongue over the sensitive points. The muscles in her belly began to quiver, her brain struggling to process that this was Easton holding her. Easton pinning her to the bed and setting her body on fire.

Shifting restlessly beneath him, she closed her eyes and let the sensation build as he switched to the other breast and slid the chemise over her hips and down her legs until she was completely naked. She lay there before him, breathing fast, her entire body alive and desperate to find out what he'd do next.

"God, you're beautiful," he whispered, cupping the side of her face as his mouth slanted across hers in a hot, intense kiss.

She wasn't beautiful but she didn't argue because she couldn't speak. The hunger had her now. A burning ache in her core that demanded satisfaction. It had been well over a year since she'd felt a man's hands on her body. Longer than that since she'd actually enjoyed sex. With Easton, she knew it would be hot and explosive. It terrified and exhilarated her all at once.

His hands were warm and sure as they moved over her naked body, tracing the shape of her, everything so much more intense than she'd ever imagined. He was giving her back her confidence, her sexuality, one touch at a time. In his arms she felt safe, worshipped and adored. The pulse between her legs was almost painful now, her sex wet and swollen and he hadn't even touched her there yet.

She stopped breathing when he slid a big hand down over her stomach to oh-so-slowly cup her mound. She groaned and lifted her hips, increasing the pressure, a silent demand for more.

Easton released her sensitive nipple and nuzzled his way down to meet his hand. His fingers slid over her slick folds, bringing thousands of nerve endings to life a moment before the warmth of his tongue stroked over her center.

"Ahh," she cried, twisting beneath him, her hands gripping his head.

He made a low sound of enjoyment as he licked at the throbbing bud of her clit, his tongue moving in a soft, slow spiral that had her eyes rolling back. His hot palms curved around the insides of her thighs, spreading them wider before closing around her hips in a firm grip that made her belly flip.

She lay there, trapped, whimpering as he licked and sucked where she needed him most. Her legs shook, the muscles in her stomach pulling tight as the tension inside her rose sharply.

As if he sensed how close she was, he stopped. She opened her eyes, a protest on her tongue but stopped and watched him strip off his jeans and underwear. He grabbed a condom and rolled it on before moving between her legs, his eyes smoldering with lust.

Desperate to touch him, she reached out and curled her hand around the thick, hot length of his erection. Easton sucked in a breath through his nose and stilled, the muscles in his abdomen and chest standing out in sharp relief. He allowed her to stroke him a few times, then made a low sound in the back of his throat and grasped her wrist to stop her.

He grabbed her hips, pulled. “Turn over.”

Dazed, more excited than she’d ever been in her life, she did as he said, rolling to her hands and knees. He tugged a pillow from the head of the bed and slid it beneath her stomach, paused to smooth his palm down the length of her spine, over the curve of her bottom.

“So gorgeous,” he whispered, kissing the curve of her shoulder. He tucked himself against her, the rigid line of his cock rubbing along her folds from behind. She bit her lip and pushed backward, wanting more, and earned a deep chuckle. “You ready for me, sweetness?”

She loved it when he called her that, his voice like dark velvet, sending goose bumps scattering over her skin. *Yes.* Beyond the ability to speak, she nodded and licked her lips, bracing her weight on her forearms. Her core clenched with the need to be filled, her entire body throbbing.

One big hand curled around her hip, holding her still. Again, the dominant grip shot another burst of arousal through her. Then the head of his cock pressed against her opening and his other hand slipped around to cup her mound, his finger sliding over her swollen clit. She shuddered at the dual sensations, the pressure and heat as he surged forward, stretching and filling her, easing the empty ache.

A soft, plaintive whimper came from her throat. She grabbed hold of the covers and held on, tried to breathe as the sensation threatened to splinter her apart.

"Oh fuck, you're so hot and tight," Easton moaned, his lips at the tender skin below her ear. A shiver rippled through her, then the hand on her hip shifted and skimmed up her body to cup her jaw. "Look at you," he whispered, his voice low, reverent.

Forcing her eyes open, she looked across the room and noticed their reflection in the large mirror atop the dresser. She caught her breath, transfixed at the picture they made.

Moonlight highlighted their bodies in beautiful strokes of silver and blue, mixing with the dark shadows.

Easton's muscular arms bunched as they surrounded her, his powerful body poised behind her. His gaze was locked on her, and the absorbed look on his face as he watched her made her insides melt. He was one-hundred percent engrossed in her, his hold so protective, focused completely on giving her pleasure.

She shivered again and automatically rocked back toward him. The feel of his erection sliding along her sensitive inner walls combined with the slow, wicked stroke of his finger over her clit. Everything in her softened, heated, surrendering to the pleasure he wrought. She trembled in his grasp, helpless under the lash of sensation, wanting more.

Still holding her jaw and her gaze, Easton growled softly and drew his hips back slightly, then surged forward. Her eyes snapped shut as he stroked over a magical spot inside her, making her see stars.

Piper moaned helplessly and rocked faster, fighting his grip, needing more of that incredible friction. He was so hot inside her, so hard, and his touch on her clit so perfect.

"Mmhmm, just like that," he whispered, his voice taut with need. He released her jaw and wrapped his arm around her ribs, anchoring her in place, and let her take what she wanted. What she needed. "So good, work that sweet spot with my cock," he rasped against the side of her neck.

Those dirty words, spoken in that dark, sexy voice, dragged a shudder out of her. Then his tongue stroked against her throat as he slid one hand up to cup her breast, fingers squeezing and tugging on her nipple. Streamers of fire shot through her body.

Oh my God...

The rise of pleasure was unbelievable, almost too much. She squeezed her eyes closed, her mouth opening as a desperate cry of need broke free. Her senses were overwhelmed with the knowledge that it was Easton touching her, Easton making her shiver and tingle all over.

Her body took over. She was nothing but pure instinct as she rocked back and forth, driving him deep inside her, using him to stroke that hidden glow inside her. His low, passion-roughened voice spoke against her ear, driving her to the edge.

The bright silver wire of sensation inside her snapped free, and she bucked as sweet oblivion took her. Desperate sobs of ecstasy echoed in her ears as her release tore through her, leaving her shattered and reborn in Easton's arms.

Chapter THIRTEEN

He'd never seen anything so fucking beautiful in his entire life as Piper letting go in his arms. A thousand times more perfect than his most vivid fantasy.

Easton gritted his teeth and tried to think of something—anything—that would distract him from the feel of being buried deep in Piper's slick heat. He'd fought like hell to make sure he outlasted her, needing to ensure she reached orgasm before he did. Without question that had been the best, most intense sex he'd ever had, and he hadn't even come yet.

When he did, he had a feeling it would destroy him, and he wanted to be looking into her face as it happened.

His breathing was rough and fast as he eased his grip on her hip, let go of the sheet he'd fisted and slowly withdrew from her body. Sweat stood out on his forehead, each square millimeter of friction sheer torture until he pulled free.

She moaned in protest, opened her eyes a little and

reached back for him. He was way past the ability to speak at the moment so rather than verbally reassure her, he gently rolled her onto her back and braced himself above her, taking a moment to smooth the hair back from her face with an unsteady hand.

She sighed and looked up at him with such trust that his heart clenched. Her eyes were drowsy, her expression satisfied. He'd put that look there. He'd made her writhe and cry out from the pleasure of his touch, made her come so hard she was too tired to move.

In the quiet with that soft, trusting look on her face, Piper raised a hand to cradle the side of his. He closed his eyes and nuzzled her palm, took a deep, shuddering breath as the need to come faded. He'd imagined this moment thousands of times and he'd be damned if he rushed through it.

As though she sensed how on edge he was, she leaned up on one elbow and drew him down to kiss her. Her arms wrapped around his shoulders and her legs twined around his hips, holding him close.

Easton moaned into her mouth and went willingly into her embrace, lowering his weight onto her. His cock rubbed against her slick folds, making his muscles twitch.

The burn in his gut spread to his groin, then throughout his entire body. He'd meant for this to last a long time, had planned to let her rest and give her another climax before seeking his own release, but the way she held him, the feel and scent of her, was too much.

Breaking the kiss, he levered his weight onto one hand and reached down to position his cock. Those hazel-green eyes glowed up at him in the moonlight, dragging him in deeper into the whirlpool of desire.

He braced his hands on either side of her head and rocked forward, slowly pushing back into her slick heat.

She made a purring sound and arched her lower back, drawing him deeper. The feel of her closing around him, that sweet, aching friction all along his swollen cock, sucked all the air out of his lungs. He fought for breath as searing hot pleasure tore through him.

Heat and pressure gathered at the base of his spine as he buried himself inside her. But the way she gazed up at him with total love in her eyes was his undoing. Piper was everything he'd ever wanted and she was finally his. He squeezed his eyes shut, pulled his hips back and surged forward.

A deep, feral sound came out of him, somewhere between a growl and a cry as he buried his face in her neck. He was all animal, gave his hunger free reign as he plunged in and out of her body, desperate for relief from the agonizing pleasure that was at once too much and not enough.

Her inner muscles squeezed him, stroking the entire length of his cock, and knowing he was buried balls deep and about to come inside Piper after all these years finished him off.

He shoved his arms beneath her back and crushed her to him, holding on like a drowning man as the brutal pleasure peaked and exploded, sending him hurtling into oblivion. His shout of release echoed in his ears along with his thundering heartbeat.

When at last it faded he sucked in a shuddering breath and relaxed his death hold on her, but couldn't move. He lay there in her embrace, destroyed.

Piper drew him closer and stroked his back, her lips skimming over his jaw, his cheek. "I don't ever want to let you go," she whispered.

Her words undid him. She hadn't said *I love you*, but it was close enough for the time being. *Then don't*, he answered silently, his brain still functioning enough to hold the words back.

"Mmmm," she murmured drowsily, and ran her hands over his damp back. She traced the muscles along his spine, followed them down to his ass and squeezed once before reversing direction and coming up to rub between his shoulder blades.

Completely wrecked, he groaned and nestled closer, soaking up the contact and intimacy of the moment.

Shit, the condom.

With effort he dragged his arms out from beneath her and pushed up onto his elbows. His arms trembled slightly as he dropped a kiss on her sexy mouth and got to his knees to ease free of her body.

His legs were weak when he stood up and went to the bathroom to deal with the condom. When he came back a minute later Piper was curled on her side waiting for him, the sheets pulled up to cover her nakedness as she watched him, an expression of pure contentment on her face.

The sight of her like that just slayed him. He wanted her in his bed every night with that exact same look on her face.

By the time he headed back to Alexandria at the end of the week, he vowed to have dispelled every last one of her insecurities about her naked body and prove to her beyond a doubt that he loved her.

He slid in next to her and immediately pulled her into his arms. She snuggled up to him with her head on his shoulder, one leg tucked between his and one arm slung around his waist.

Skimming a hand over the silken curve of her spine, her heart beating steady against his, Easton took in a contented breath and released it on a satisfied sigh.

"In case you couldn't tell, I really enjoyed that," Piper murmured against his skin.

He smiled into her hair. "Me too."

"No, like *really*."

A low chuckle escaped him. "Yeah, me too."

"I'm looking forward to doing that again later. Right after I sleep for a while."

"I love sleeping next to you."

She shifted in his arms and tipped her head back to look into his face. "I love it too."

"Then don't go." The words were out before he could stop them, his heart laid bare to her.

She stared at him for a long moment, and he saw the pain in her eyes before she stiffened and looked away. "Easton…"

He couldn't let it go. She meant too much to him and he couldn't live without her. "Don't go back to Minnesota. Stay with me."

She shook her head. "I have to. I already took the job. My dream job."

"So call them and tell them you changed your mind and we'll find you your dream job somewhere near Alexandria."

She blinked and looked back at him. "Alexandria?"

"Yeah. I know it's still Virginia, but it's far away enough from Sugar Hollow to give you a fresh start."

He could see the indecision warring in her eyes before she responded. "And what about your job? You're gone all the time, sometimes for months."

"Maybe that's the key to a perfect relationship—me being out of your hair for months at a time."

Her lips quirked, then her expression turned serious. "I've always worried about you when you're at work, and that was before we got…together."

He wasn't going to lie and tell her his job wasn't dangerous. Even his training was, and there was no guarantee he'd be safe. "I could get killed driving through Sugar Hollow, too."

She gasped and put her fingers over his mouth. "Don't say things like that," she said with a fierce scowl.

He kissed her fingers and eased her hand away. “Well, I could. Does my job bother you so much that you’d be willing to walk away from us?”

“No,” she murmured.

His lungs started working again and he relaxed. “I don’t know how many years I have left on the team, but I don’t plan to do this job forever. I’m good at it and I love the guys on my team.”

“I know, and I wouldn’t ask you to quit because of me.”

“I realize it’s not easy, being with someone like me, but I know you’re strong enough to handle it. I think I’ll just know when it’s time for me to step aside and do something else.”

She was quiet for a long moment, stroking his chest with her fingertips, and he knew she was thinking about the job in Minnesota. It was a deal breaker for her. Dammit. “Can we not talk about this anymore for tonight?” she murmured. “Please?”

Patience. She wasn’t telling him no. He had to give her just a little more time and maybe, maybe he could convince her not to go. “You wanna sleep on it?”

“Yes.”

“Well too bad, because I don’t plan to let you sleep much.” He rolled her onto her back, plunged his hands into the cool silk of her hair and leaned down to kiss that smiling mouth.

Chapter FOURTEEN

"Got enough food here to feed a freaking army," Easton said with a grunt as he loaded the last of the groceries into the backseat of his truck.

"Ha, not quite. But I'm well acquainted with how you guys eat, so I wanted to make sure I had plenty." She was glad to be alone with him for a little while, even if it was just to run for groceries.

He'd been out all day with his buddy Jamie, at her insistence, giving her time to mull everything over and just relax, and shown up at the cabin an hour ago covered in mud from head to toe after a day of dirt biking, grinning like a kid. Still a hell raiser and adrenaline junkie underneath all that tenderness he'd shown her.

Easton felt she was safe enough to go with him to get groceries, but since there was a risk that people might still be watching for her, they'd driven to the next town over to buy everything. She'd insisted on paying for it all herself. Money was tight right now, true, but as soon as her place sold she'd be debt free, and she couldn't have done it without Easton and his family's support.

The police had called earlier that afternoon to tell her they had no further information on Greg. No one even knew if he was still alive. The only update was that there had been apparent sightings of Gallant down near the Tennessee border, and the possibility that he was so far away from Sugar Hollow eased some of her anxiety.

She'd also fielded another tearful call from her ex-mother-in-law, even though she desperately wanted more distance from them, Greg, and this entire situation. Her heart went out to them, which was why she'd answered. She'd tried to give the woman what comfort she could, but it wasn't much.

"You didn't have to do all this." Easton opened her door for her.

"I know, but I wanted to. It's the least I could do to thank all of you for everything you've done to help me. Besides, you know I like to cook for a crowd every now and then. I've been feeling antsy not being in my kitchen for the past week."

"I dunno how you think we're gonna eat all this."

She shrugged. "So there'll be some leftovers. Better too much than not enough. And let's not forget I'm making all your favorites."

At that he grinned at her from across the cab. "If you're going with the whole 'the way to a man's heart is through his stomach' thing, it's overkill. You've already got all of me."

"We'll call this insurance then," she said, carefully sidestepping the issue and giving him a playful smile. She hadn't said the words back to him yet but he must know how she felt and he was being so patient with her.

Even though she loved him, it wasn't fair to say it unless she was going to stay in Virginia. All day she'd thought about his offer, about moving with him to Alexandria. Part of her loved the idea and part of her balked at giving up her dream job and taking such a huge step so soon.

She also couldn't stop thinking about last night, and about the possibility of a future with Easton. Could it really work out for them long term if she stayed? Waking up beside him when he was home was a tantalizing prospect.

He'd captured every bit of her heart last night, but she wasn't sure it was enough to sustain them if she moved so far away.

Nervousness and excitement bubbled inside her as she thought about what would happen tonight, after dinner when they were alone in the cabin. But with a big meal to prep and cook and most of his family around while she did it, she wouldn't be comfortable touching or kissing him the way she was dying to. It was all so new, she wanted to give everyone time to adjust to the idea of her and Easton being together before she groped and mauled him in public.

Not touching or tasting him all day was slowly driving her crazy though. Piper snuck glances at him as he drove, while a country station played on the radio. Just looking at him made her hot. The arousal kept building until she had to shift in her seat to relieve the ache between her thighs.

It didn't help. She kept remembering what he'd done to her last night, the way he'd laid her completely bare and given her such incredible pleasure. She wanted more of it, that special connection between them, and to bask in the security of his love. She also wanted the chance to explore him without the searing ache of her own need in the way.

Studying his strong profile as he drove along a country road, she couldn't stop from reaching out to trail her fingers down the side of his cheek. He smiled and without taking his eyes off the road, caught her hand to kiss each fingertip, pausing to suck each one.

He's mine.

The incredible thought almost made her light-headed. She wanted to peel his clothes off right now and use her mouth to make him insane. The dinner prep could wait a while longer.

Undoing her seatbelt, she leaned over the console and kissed the edge of that tempting mouth.

"Hey, no distracting me while I drive," he said on a laugh.

"Okay, so pull over."

He glanced at her in surprise. "Are you serious?"

"Yes. Pull over. Right now." She kissed her way down his jaw to his neck, scraped her teeth there gently while letting her hands roam over his shoulders and chest, down his tensing abdomen and to the bulge behind the zipper of his jeans.

A low groan rumbled from him when she curled her hand around his trapped erection and squeezed before rubbing it with her palm. "You're gonna cause an accident."

She trailed her tongue up the side of his neck, enjoying herself immensely, getting drunk on the feel of him and the anticipation of tasting him. It had become one of her favorite fantasies over the past few days, to go down on him and make him lose his mind. Sexy Easton Colebrook, at her mercy and loving every second of it.

"So you'd better hurry up and get us off the road." She unhooked his belt and slid the leather through the buckle.

With a low chuckle he took the next turn and found an access road that led to a farmer's field just as she undid the button at the top of his fly. Tall grass bordered either side, sheltering them from view from the road beyond.

He pulled up far enough to give them privacy, then parked and shut off the ignition. Before he could undo his own seatbelt she had his zipper down and her hand inside his underwear, wrapping her fingers around him.

He growled in approval and reached for her, plunging a hand into her hair and fisting tight to bring her mouth up to his. The kiss was hot and carnal, so different from the gentle tenderness of last night.

A tiny shiver rippled through her at the evidence of his hunger for her. He was rock hard in her grip, hot and swollen as she stroked him with her fist, earning a moan from him. She sucked at his tongue, hungry to do the same to his cock and show him everything she felt for him.

Pulling her mouth free, she let her lips glide down the side of his neck and scooted up on her knees to lean over him. His cock pulsed in her hand, making her core clench.

His hand tightened in her hair and he sucked in a quick breath when he realized her intent. "Piper."

She didn't answer, didn't stop, too caught up in what she was doing. The sight of him so hard for her made her feel powerful and desired, swelled her heart with love. Bending toward his lap, she paused to nuzzle the muscles in his abdomen, felt them contract beneath her cheek an instant before she rubbed her lips over the engorged crown of his cock.

"Oh, fuck," he moaned, his hips lifting in an almost helpless motion when she ran her tongue around him.

Her heart galloped, the need to pleasure him taking over. Parting her lips, she took him into her mouth and swirled her tongue around him, tasting his sharp, salty flavor.

"Oh God, sweetness…" His voice trailed off into a throaty growl that stirred her up even more.

The velvet rasp of his voice, the raw enjoyment in it, turned her on even more. She worked him slow and firm, learning what he liked, taking as much of him as she could without gagging. His thigh muscles twitched beneath her free hand and his breathing turned erratic.

Her own body responded in kind, breasts swelling, nipples tightening and that empty ache building between her thighs. The only sounds in the truck cab were his rough groans and the wet sounds of her mouth as she sucked him.

He cradled the back of her head with his free hand and released her hair, smoothing his hand down her back and over her upturned bottom. Grabbing the frilly hem of her dress, he eased it up to her hips then slid his hand along her sensitized skin, skimming the curve of her rear and the back of her thigh before trailing up the inside to brush over the front of her panties. She gasped and rocked into his touch, her entire body on fire.

Pulsing all over, she pulled her mouth free and clambered over the console to straddle him. His arms clamped around her ribs and hips, holding her flush against him as she sought his mouth. She kissed him with every bit of pent up passion she'd lived with these past few lonely years, rubbed her body along his, making the ache between her thighs worse.

"Please say you have a condom," she breathed against his lips.

"Yeah," he managed. He released her ribs and raised his hips enough to fish out his wallet, but the pressure of his erection against her aching core made her whimper.

She snatched it from him, tore it open and leaned back to smooth it down the length of his erection. He reached beneath her dress and grabbed the edge of her panties, ripping them with one savage yank.

She stared at him in surprise for a moment, then let out a laugh and went back for more of his mouth, tasting and teasing him with her tongue. She didn't give him the chance to do anything else, just gripped his shoulders and shifted on her knees to rub her slick folds against the hot length of his cock. Easton's eyes were heavy-lidded as he watched her, his hands settling on her waist, fingers squeezing deep.

The friction felt so good, but she wanted more, wanted to ride him and stare at his face while he came apart for her. She slid up, her thigh muscles quivering as she slowly lowered herself onto him. The heat and pressure made her gasp. Her eyes fluttered shut as the thickness of him penetrated, stretching her, stroking all those secret, deliciously tingling nerve endings.

Ohhhh... She bit her lip at the delectable fullness.

A low, rough growl reverberated in his chest. She opened her eyes to find him staring at her, his jaw tense and nostrils flared, his velvet-brown eyes almost black with hunger. His arms contracted around her, holding her tighter. *Tighter*. As though he couldn't get close enough.

Pure feminine power rippled through her, blending with the tendrils of pleasure coiling deep in her abdomen. She felt beautiful, strong and sexy as she began to ride him. It had been so long since she'd felt that way, and Easton certainly was helping restore her confidence. This man owned her already, body and heart.

He hissed in a breath and closed his eyes, sensual agony stamped on every feature as his head fell back against the headrest. "Oh, Jesus, Piper…"

She loved that he needed her so much, that she was making him feel so good. "I want to watch you," she whispered back, fascinated, hungry for more. "I want to watch you when I make you come."

He shuddered, his hands squeezing her waist. He was so damn gorgeous like this, allowing her to take control, and the feel of him inside her made her want to purr in satisfaction.

She rode him a little faster, her eager gaze devouring every detail of his reaction. The tightening of his facial muscles, the way his throat worked as he swallowed. Every slick, hot glide stoked the fire inside her and soon she couldn't stand it. She slipped a hand between her legs and stroked the taut bundle of nerves begging for touch.

A look of raw hunger came over his face and he released her waist to undo the halter tie at the back of her neck. She arched her back as the fabric fell away and his hands pulled the cups of her bra down to expose her aching breasts.

On a groan of pure need, he leaned forward to take one nipple into his mouth and the sudden lash of pleasure made her cry out. Her entire body tightened. She grabbed the back of his head and kept stroking herself as she slid up and down the hot, hard length of his cock. He sucked at her, his tongue like warm velvet as he stroked her captive flesh.

The heat and tension rose sharply, shocking her with the sudden intensity. Within a minute her legs were shaking, her inner walls contracting as her orgasm loomed. Her moans filled the cab as it hit, mixing with his deeper groan, his hands holding her steady.

Gasping for breath as she opened her eyes, she pulled her hand from between her thighs and gripped his shoulders for balance. His face was tight, his entire body rigid with unrelieved tension. A sheen of sweat glistened on his forehead. He was still hot and hard inside her.

Realization hit. She'd wanted to watch him and he'd held back to make sure she could. Tenderness flooded her.

Moving slower now, she pumped her hips and took his face between her hands, all her focus on him. After one slow, erotic kiss that had him moaning into her mouth, she eased back and watched his face as she took him to heaven.

Easton leaned his head back, jaw clenched as he stared directly into her eyes. His breathing was erratic, the pulse in his throat going crazy as she rode him with slow, lazy strokes. She'd imagined doing this to him so many times, and finally being able to make fantasy reality was so much better than she'd expected.

She knew the moment he reached the point of no return. His eyes went hazy an instant before they slammed shut and he swelled impossibly thicker inside her. Those delectable lips parted and a long, ragged groan ripped free, his hands biting into her hips as he drove up into her and shuddered with his release.

I love you. The words were right there, right on the tip of her tongue. She bit them back. She would *not* say them while she still intended to move away. But at least she'd shown him.

With a deep, contented sigh a few minutes later he opened his eyes and looked at her, his breathing still a little ragged. "That was so fucking hot."

A smug smile tugged at her lips. "I know."

He burst out a laugh and slid his hands into her hair, tugging her forward into a kiss so full of love and tenderness it brought tears to her eyes. And right then, she knew.

Walking away from this man would rip her heart out. So what the hell was she going to do?

Chapter FIFTEEN

"Well, I'd say that was a hit." Easton came up behind her as she set an empty serving platter on the counter beside the sink and wrapped his arms around her, bending to nuzzle the side of her neck.

She stiffened even as tingles raced across her skin, then felt horrible. Everyone else was still in the dining room and couldn't see them. She didn't want him to think she was embarrassed or ashamed, it was just that this was all so new and she felt a little uncomfortable at the idea of his family seeing them.

"I'm glad. And see? There's not as much left over as you thought there would be. You boys can eat."

"It's because we haven't tasted anything so delicious before," he murmured against her neck, then sucked lightly, making it clear he meant more than the food. She shivered.

"Hey, none of that," a deep voice said behind them.

She gasped and looked back to see Wyatt carrying in

an armful of empty plates. Embarrassed, without thinking she slipped out of Easton's embrace, her face growing hot. The second she did, she regretted her reaction. Easton had done nothing wrong, yet she'd pulled away as if Wyatt had walked in on them feeling each other up or something.

Wyatt stepped past them and she glanced over at Easton. His expression was set, hurt and annoyance clear in his eyes. *Dammit.*

She cleared her throat. "Could you go grab the rest of the food so we can wrap it up?" she asked him.

"Sure." His voice was clipped and she inwardly winced as he turned and walked out of the kitchen.

Blowing out a breath, she glanced at Wyatt, who was studiously ignoring her as he stacked the plates in the sink. "Can I talk to you for a minute? Alone?" She couldn't put this conversation off any longer.

He met her gaze, his hazel eyes full of understanding. "Sure. Come on."

She followed him out the back door and around the side of the house, where they'd have more privacy. He stopped and faced her, hands in his pockets, and waited for her to speak. She rubbed a hand over the back of her neck, not sure where to begin. "So I guess Easton told you about…things."

"He told us the way he felt about you. I didn't know if it was mutual or not."

"It is."

"Good. I was hoping it would be."

She looked up at him in surprise, the twilight illuminating the scars on his face. It was like he was carved from granite. Solid. Unmovable. He'd been through so much, had overcome so much. She'd been there for him as much as she could—as much as he'd allowed her to be. And sometimes she'd been there whether he'd wanted her to be or not. "Really?"

He nodded, the hint of a smile playing around the edges of his mouth. "If you're happy then I'm happy. And I'm glad to see him wanting to settle down."

That part scared her a little, as it seemed too big a change for someone with Easton's hell-raiser reputation to suddenly be the guy who wanted to settle down and have her move in with him. She definitely wanted to see where things went though. "So it's not…weird for you?"

He shrugged his wide shoulders. "I'll adjust. We all will. Don't worry about that."

At his words, the tightness in her stomach eased. She laughed softly. "Okay. It's an adjustment for me too." Her gaze strayed back toward the kitchen window. "I think I hurt his feelings just now. I didn't mean to."

"He'll get over it."

He shouldn't have to get over it. She felt terrible for the way she'd reacted. Facing Wyatt once more, she drank in the sight of his dear, scarred face, a fond smile tugging at her lips.

Wyatt stepped closer and pulled her into a tight hug, pressing his cheek to the top of her head. "Be happy. And if my little brother doesn't treat you right, I'll pound the shit out of him for you."

She laughed. "Thanks. I'm hoping that won't be necessary." More likely, she was the one who was going to hurt Easton if she took the job in Minnesota.

He straightened and his expression sobered, those hazel eyes direct, intent. "Whatever happens between you two, you'll always be family to us. No matter what."

Her throat tightened. "Thanks."

He squeezed her once, then released her and clapped a friendly hand on her shoulder. "Well? Better get back in there and make him stop sulking."

****

Easton strode back into the dining room to get the last of the plates from the table, still stinging from Piper's rejection.

It annoyed him that he was hurt over something so small, but the way she'd yanked away from him the moment his brother had stepped into the kitchen made it clear she was either embarrassed or uncomfortable about having their relationship out in the open. Neither of those reasons were okay with him.

He reached across the table to grab the nearly empty bowl of mashed potatoes and glanced at the window. What the hell were she and Wyatt talking about out there, anyway?

Charlie helped him clear and followed him back into the kitchen, leaving their dad, Jamie and Austen to continue their lively conversation.

"What's the matter?" she asked, frowning at him as she set everything on the counter.

"Nothing."

The back door opened and Wyatt stepped inside, Grits right on his heels. He gave Easton a little smile on the way by that said everything was okay and the tension he hadn't even realized he'd been carrying bled out of his shoulders. Then Piper came in and he stilled. She met his gaze as she shut the door behind her, then flicked a glance at Charlie.

His sister glanced between the two of them, got the message, and turned on her heel to leave the room. Easton shoved his hands into his pockets. "What did you guys talk about?"

"Us." She walked over to him, slid her arms around his waist and leaned up on her toes to kiss him. "I'm sorry. I didn't mean to pull away, I just reacted without thinking."

Sighing, he slid his hands out of his pockets to hug her. "I don't want to hide this. I can't, because I love you and I won't pretend I don't."

"I know." Her eyes were full of regret, and the love she was too scared to profess yet. It was enough. "I'm not embarrassed of us. This is all new and I didn't handle that well. I really am sorry. You're so important to me, and I don't want to ruin this."

Snagging her hand, he turned around and started walking toward the dining room.

"What are you doing?" she asked, trailing behind him.

He stopped in the entrance of the dining room and tugged Piper forward until she was standing next to him, then wrapped an arm around her waist and pulled her into his side. Making it plain as day what the situation was. Five pairs of eyes stared at them.

"Piper and I are officially together," he announced. "So you guys can just deal with seeing me kiss her."

Piper made a choked sound but didn't protest when he slid a hand into her hair and bent to kiss her. Her eyes were wide as he leaned down and sealed his mouth over hers. He heard Jamie's low chuckle, then Charlie and Austen both cheered and clapped.

When he lifted his head a moment later Piper stared up at him, her cheeks bright pink. "There. Secret that wasn't really a secret is out."

"Well, that's one way to do it," Wyatt muttered, and when Easton looked over at him, he was shaking his head in dismay.

But there was one person's approval that mattered to him more than anyone else's. He shifted his gaze to his father, who was staring at them with an unreadable expression.

"Dad?" Beside him, he could feel Piper holding her breath as she awaited his father's reaction. "Tell her you're fine with it. She'll worry otherwise."

A lopsided grin split his father's face, filled with such

approval and affection that Easton's chest tightened. "'Bout damn time."

Everyone laughed and Piper hid her face against his chest, but not before he caught the relieved smile there. He hugged her to him and kissed the top of her head. "See? Nothing to worry about. We're good."

She nodded, let out a shaky laugh. "I'm going to punish you later for this. Severely."

"Oooh, can't wait."

"Pervert." She tipped her head back to glare up at him, but her eyes were brimming with a mix of annoyance and laughter. "I thought you said you'd matured."

"Well, no one's perfect," he said with a grin. "But if anyone can tame me, it's you." And now that he'd gone and made a spectacle of them, he needed to get her out of here and give her time to decompress.

Staking his claim in front of his family was one thing; embarrassing her was another. "Come on, let's go dig your clothes out of the shed."

****

This is a really shitty plan. The kind that could get him killed.

He had no choice but to go through with it, however.

Greg kept his breathing shallow in an effort to spare his cracked ribs as he crouched down and knelt in the underbrush of the heavy woods at the far west side of the Colebrook property. Gallant stood a few feet behind him with a 9 mm Beretta aimed at his back, and two of his goons stood off to either side. They all wore NVGs to help them see in the growing darkness.

Everything hurt, inside and out. He'd pissed blood this morning, right after receiving the beating and the kidney shots that had gotten him to agree to do this.

Even during his worst days in the Army, nothing had been this bad.

"How far away is the shed?" Gallant asked him.

He let out a slow, painful breath before answering. "Through the woods and across the pasture. Few hundred yards maybe." In his condition, that was going to feel like a few miles and he dreaded each and every step he'd have to take. He was better trained than the others.

A small part of him wanted to run, to risk getting shot in the back and just take off into the forest. He knew the area. Knew how to hide and evade someone tracking him. He also knew it would be suicide. At his prime, he might have been able to do it. The pain would slow him too much, and he was weak. They'd either catch him or shoot him before he'd made it five steps.

It had been months since he'd had a hit of anything stronger than coffee, and man, what he wouldn't give for the chance at oblivion right now.

At this point, he'd decided that death might be a blessing. But if he died it would leave Piper in serious danger. That was the only reason he stayed put. He had to pull this off, find what he'd stolen from Gallant, and hope it was enough. After that, he didn't care what happened to him. Just as long as Piper didn't suffer any more for his sins.

He'd been a shitty person, and an even shittier husband. He'd allowed the addiction to take over his life and transform him into someone even he hadn't recognized. Half-assed attempts at getting clean over the past few years had done nothing to clean him up.

He'd thought his rock bottom moment was when Piper had left him. He'd come home one day to find the house empty, all her clothes and belongings gone. No note, not even a text to tell him. She'd finally up and left him as she'd been threatening to do for the last two years of their marriage, leaving the signed separation papers on the kitchen counter for him to find.

On the one hand while he didn't blame her for that, it had still crushed him. He'd wound up going on a week-long bender. Didn't remember anything after that third hit, until he'd woken up in the hospital with the doctors telling him he was lucky to be alive.

This rock bottom was so much worse. His actions had not only endangered his life, but now Piper's as well. He had to fix this. Protect her however he could. He owed her that much.

"Dawson says there are four trucks and an SUV out front of the house," Gallant said to him in a quiet voice. He gave the makes and models. "Know who they belong to?"

"No." This was fucking insane. Old man Colebrook would be there, along with Easton and whoever else was staying at the house.

Gallant and his men hadn't been trained by the military. They had no discipline, and worse, were unpredictable because they had nothing to lose and Gallant had made it clear he was willing to kill whoever he had to in order to recoup his lost goods.

"Get moving," Gallant ordered, gesturing impatiently with the pistol.

"What if it's not even there?" he asked, trying one last time to make Gallant call this off.

"Then we'll take Piper and convince her to remember where the furniture is. Now *move*, asshole."

The things they would do to Piper made Greg's blood run cold. He had to keep her safe. God knew he'd failed her in every other way; he couldn't fail her now.

Chapter SIXTEEN

"So I see subtlety still isn't one of your strong points," Piper joked to Easton as they headed through the barn hand-in-hand, torn between annoyance and laughter.

"Well now you don't have to feel shy about us anymore." He raised her hand to his lips and kissed the back of it, as if that made it all better.

"You're lucky I'm so into you, otherwise I'd be really pissed right now."

He stopped and turned to face her, the overhead lights in the barn illuminating the strong planes of his face as he looked down at her. Several horses were in the stalls, mostly expectant mothers. One stomped its hoof against the floor and another snorted out a long breath.

"Guess that means I dodged another bullet," he murmured, and lowered his mouth to hers. The kiss was slow at first, tender, then harder. Possessive.

When he raised his head a minute later, she was dazed and breathless. He studied her eyes, and a satisfied grin curved his lips. "And now I know how to make up with you when you're mad at me."

She snickered at his self-satisfied expression. "As long as you don't take advantage of it or make it a habit, I'm okay with that."

"That's fair. Now let's go get you some clothes." He waggled his eyebrows. "Although I find the thought of you running around the cabin naked pretty appealing."

"Ha, no. You wish. Pervert." She'd die of embarrassment if Mr. C or anyone else happened to catch sight of her as she darted from room to room.

His eyes gleamed with hunger as he smiled at her. "You love it."

Okay, yeah. She did.

Looking all too smug at her lack of retort, he tugged on her hand and they continued out the back door of the barn. Thin clouds drifted over the half moon and a damp, dew-scented breeze ruffled her hair.

The shed was painted to match the barn, situated a stone's throw from the back entrance. It housed gardening tools and the ride-on lawnmower, as well as all her remaining clothes and the few pieces of furniture she'd packed away with the boxes.

As soon as they stepped out onto the gravel path that connected the barn and shed, Sarge pushed himself to his feet where he'd been napping against the barn. The old basset hound set his front paws out in front of his long body and gave a mighty, shuddering stretch, his butt and tail pointing skyward, then trotted after them.

Easton undid the padlock holding the door shut and flipped on the light. The twenty-by-twenty shed was stacked to the roof with her things. "Where are the ones with your clothes?" he asked, maneuvering his way through the stacks of cardboard boxes.

"I don't remember but most of them should be labeled." In her haste she hadn't been as careful or organized as she normally would have.

"Of course they are," he murmured.

She shot him a look. "Just look around until you find them. I'll start here." She stepped up to the closest one and ripped the packing tape off.

"Here. Try this." Easton leaned over a stack of boxes to hand her a wickedly-sharp military-style blade, handle first. "Careful with it. It's like a razor."

She took it, blinked at him. "Where did it come from?" He was only wearing jeans and a T-shirt, plus his holster. The sheath must be hidden under one of the legs of his jeans.

His eyes held a mischievous twinkle. "I'll let you search me later and find out."

"All right, I'm game for that." Smiling to herself, she sliced through the tape without any effort, and carefully set the knife on top of another box while she opened the first one. Towels, her pretty soaps and other toiletries met her gaze. "Nope. Not this one." She folded the flaps together to lock them in place and set it aside, shook the next one to test for weight. The quiet clink of dishes answered what was in it.

Easton was already working his way through a stack of boxes on the other side of the shed. "Think I've got something here. Oh yeah," he murmured, holding up a fistful of ruby red lace.

She blushed and opened her mouth to tell him to put it back but he shook it out and let the sexy chemise dangle by the straps from his hand. "You can wear this while you're searching me," he added, looking pleased with himself. "I wonder what else you've got in here?" He ducked his head and rummaged through the box some more. "Oh, man. I'm so glad I didn't know you had a lingerie obsession all these years. It might have killed me."

"You're such a dork," she said on a laugh and opened

the next box. She finally found one containing something to wear over her lingerie hoard and dug through it to find some warmer items.

Sarge was sniffing around near her feet. She stepped out of his way and he disappeared through the maze of boxes to go search along the side of the shed, where all the furniture was.

"You find anything?" When Easton didn't answer, she heard a soft *woof* and looked up. He was staring at something she couldn't see, presumably Sarge, and the intent expression on his face made her pulse quicken. "What is it?"

"Look at him," he said, pushing boxes aside to make a path for himself.

Piper hurried to do the same. After clearing enough room to squeeze through, she stepped around a stack of boxes and found Sarge sitting at the foot of one of her grandmother's pieces. He was perfectly still, gazing up at Easton. "He's not doing anything."

"I think maybe he's alerting. Get Wyatt." Easton bent to examine the small chest of drawers.

Her eyes widened. Sarge was a retired narcotics and tracking dog.

Whirling, she rushed out of the shed and ran to the house. "Wyatt," she called out as soon as she threw the back door open. "Easton thinks Sarge is alerting him about something in the shed. Can you come check?"

He was there in moments, jogging with her back to the shed. Easton was stretched out on his belly with a small flashlight out, studying the back of the chest. He looked up at Wyatt. "He was sniffing around, circling it, then just sat all of a sudden and woofed once. He hasn't moved away from this spot."

"Let me see," Wyatt said, easing past her to squeeze in beside his brother. "Sarge. Search," he said, pointing at the chest.

The old basset came to life before her eyes, tail wagging as he snuffled at the back of the piece of furniture, then sat, back ramrod straight, and looked up at Wyatt.

"Yeah, he's got something."

Piper stood off to the side and watched them work, hands on her cheeks. Oh God, had Greg hidden drugs in there all this time? What kind and how many? Her heart beat faster as she waited for them to find it. Just another disappointment when it came to her ex.

"I'll be damned," Easton muttered.

"What?" she asked, moving closer. Wyatt was crouched down beside his brother, eyes glued to something at the back of it.

"False panel," Wyatt said.

No way. She'd emptied it and packed it over here, then she and Easton had checked it out again the other night. "Where?"

"Right here." Wyatt aimed the beam of the flashlight to where Easton was working.

"Hand me my knife, Pipe."

She gave it to him, knelt on the opposite side so she didn't get in the way while he worked. He gently pried one edge of a thin sheet of mahogany away from the back of the chest. It creaked ominously and she instinctively winced before reminding herself no one cared about a damn antique when the solution to Greg's kidnapping might be inside it. Besides, Austen could fix it if it broke.

Easton worked up the seam of the wood, carefully easing it away from the back and to her surprise she found herself wanting to snap at him to hurry and to hell with being careful of the wood. She appreciated that he was being so careful with something that meant so much to her. He worked all four corners loose and pried the thin, flat board free.

All three of them leaned closer to see what was inside.

"Ah, shit," Easton murmured, and her heart sank. He reached in and pulled out brick-shaped packages wrapped in black plastic and secured with duct tape. Then a bag, and a flash drive.

He opened the bag, and she couldn't help but gasp. Thick stacks of hundred dollar bills filled it. And Easton just kept pulling out more. "Oh my God." It was an obscene amount of money. How had Greg fit it all in there?

"Gotta be over a hundred kay here, easy." He opened one of the bricks and her stomach twisted when she saw the white powder.

"Cocaine," she said, feeling hollow inside.

"Yeah." He looked up at her, his face grave. "No wonder he's in such deep shit. The amount in here has to be worth another hundred kay in street value, maybe more. And who the hell knows what's on this flash drive." He handed it over to her, along with a passport.

She took the items even though she didn't want to, and opened the passport. Greg's picture hit her like a punch to the stomach, as did his false name and information. "It's fake."

Easton got to his knees, watching her. "He was planning to run. This was his insurance if he ever needed to get out of the country."

Piper stared at the items in her hands as a sense of unreality hit her. "I swear to God I feel like I never even knew who he was."

"Not your fault," he reminded her, reaching out to run a hand over the back of her hair. "He did this behind your back, putting you in a shitload of risk."

Cold seeped into her. How could he have done this to her? Hidden this shit in one of her cherished heirlooms and kept it in their home all this time?

It shouldn't have surprised her, but it did. She was so glad she had Easton now, instead of still being saddled to Greg.

He pushed to his feet, leaving Wyatt to grab everything he'd emptied onto the floor, and took her hand. "I'm betting it's encrypted. Come on. Let's take this inside and see if Charlie can work some magic on it."

She followed him back to the house and stood there in a daze while Wyatt laid out everything on the dining room table. The others gaped at it all as Easton gave Charlie the flash drive.

Charlie opened up her laptop and got to work, calling two of her co-workers to help her de-encrypt the drive. "He sure didn't want anyone to find out what was on here," she murmured, typing away, eyes on the screen.

"There we go."

Easton and Jamie moved nearer to her. Piper stepped close to Easton as he braced both hands on the edge of the table and leaned toward the laptop.

Numbers appeared on the screen and nothing else. No names. No address.

"What are they?" Piper asked.

"Not sure yet," Charlie said. "Hang on." She called someone else back in D.C. and asked them to run the numbers through their system at work. Within minutes the person called back and Charlie input the numbers through a program she had. "There we go."

On screen, the website for a bank in the Cayman Islands came up. Piper put a hand over her mouth, disbelief crashing through her. He'd had access to an offshore account and she hadn't even known about it? What had he been doing? Running drugs? Laundering money?

Easton glanced over his shoulder at her, saw her expression and immediately straightened to slide a hand around her waist. "It's gonna be okay," he murmured, pulling her close to him. "We just need to know exactly what we're dealing with here before we alert the cops."

"This is so much worse than I ever imagined," she said in a shaky voice, her throat tight. The backs of her eyes burned. Greg wasn't worth her tears, but this was so unbelievable. The level of deceit, the depths of his corruption, were too much.

Easton didn't respond, just kissed her temple and kept her close while Charlie tried to hack into the bank's system with help from her pals back at the office. Sooner than Piper had imagined, they'd broken into the account under the name listed on Greg's false passport. What they'd just done was illegal but at the moment she couldn't bring herself to care.

"Whoa, holy shit," Charlie breathed. Now everyone was gathered around the laptop, including Austen and Mr. C.

Piper's eyes widened as she looked at the screen. "Are those…dollar amounts?"

"US dollars, yeah."

Piper scanned them quickly, a mix of shock and revulsion making her stomach churn. She counted hundreds of thousands of dollars as she added the numbers up. It was four times what Greg had racked up in debt while they'd been married. He'd had the means to pay it all off at any time, and yet he'd instead hidden it all away in the offshore account she'd been unaware of, and unable to touch.

"Is it from his parents, maybe?" Charlie asked her. "Maybe he socked away various amounts they gave him over time?"

Piper shook her head. "They cut him off financially years ago. This…he had to have gotten it illegally." She swallowed and looked at Easton for help.

He was watching the screen. "My gut says it's from

Gallant, or at least from his network. Greg got in over his head and got desperate. He knew they'd come after him so he'd been socking this away and hid the package in the chest of drawers for collateral."

It was unreal. "How did he get the money?"

Easton exchanged a loaded glance with Jamie before answering. "He must have skimmed money and product from Gallant or someone further up the chain. Maybe he'd embezzled money, too. It's hard to say."

Her head was spinning. The depth of Greg's betrayal rocked her to the core. "We need to call the police." She didn't want him to die. She wanted to find out the truth, and for him to be held accountable for what he'd done.

"I'll do it." Easton pulled out his phone and walked into the kitchen to make the call.

While everyone else spoke in hushed tones of shock and disbelief, Piper stared at the drugs, money and passport sitting on the table. She wanted to move it somewhere else, because the sight of it tainted this room, and the beautiful family gathered around the old table where they'd shared so many meals together.

Easton's low, deep voice carried to her from the kitchen. She turned away from the others and the damning evidence on the table and headed toward him. Right now she was numb, lost. She needed him to be her anchor through the coming storm.

He saw her come in, reached out an arm for her and wrapped it around her, holding her to his broad chest. She closed her eyes and leaned her forehead on his pectoral muscle, breathing in his clean, masculine scent. Maybe the police would be able to track down Gallant and negotiate for Greg's release now.

You're not that naïve anymore, Piper. You know he's going to die.

She curled her fingers into the soft cotton of Easton's shirt and let out a hard sigh. She didn't want to think of what would happen to Greg now, or how Bea and John would react to this latest news. She just wanted this nightmare to end so she could finally move forward with her life, once and for all.

"Sounds good. See you soon." Easton ended the call and slipped his phone back into his pocket before sliding both arms around her back and hugging her tight. "The detectives and investigative team will be over within the hour."

She nodded without moving her forehead from his chest. "So what now?"

"We should go take another look at the rest of what you've got in the shed. There might be more."

Deflated but resigned to face what was coming, she straightened. "Okay."

The air felt cold on her skin as she stepped out into the darkness to follow Easton back to the shed, Sarge waddling beside them. She shivered, then Sarge stopped and stared intently at something in the darkness that she couldn't see. The fur on his back stood up and he let out a deep snarl that made the back of her neck prickle.

Easton's body was rigid beside her. He stared in the direction Sarge was looking and reached out one arm to grab her and push her behind him.

The moment he did a gunshot rang out, shattering the stillness.

Chapter SEVENTEEN

Piper didn't even have time to flinch before Easton spun around and tackled her to the ground.

Fear sucked the air from her lungs, made her entire body rigid as she lay pressed into the ground beneath Easton's weight. Sharp bits of gravel dug into her but she didn't dare move, didn't make a sound.

"Get to the barn," he commanded gruffly, rolling off her and yanking her to her feet. She stumbled, took a jerky step forward. "*Run*." He shoved her in the direction he wanted her to go, sent her lurching a few steps toward the barn.

She sent him an uncertain glance as he drew his gun from the holster at his hip but then did as he said, her heart in her throat as her feet flew over the ground. That shot had come out of nowhere. She hadn't seen the shooter, didn't know how many there were or what was happening.

The breath sawed in and out of her lungs as she raced for the barn, her skin crawling, waiting for a bullet to tear through her flesh. Easton's running footsteps crunched over the gravel behind her.

The back door of the house burst open and Wyatt's deep voice called out. "You guys okay?"

"Yeah. Shot came from the west, I think," Easton answered.

Wyatt cursed and the door banged shut.

"Get down and stay low," Easton said to her, his quiet voice cutting through the panic inside her. With his back to the wall he began inching his way toward the rear door of the barn.

She wanted to tell him to stop, to stay here with her, but she was afraid to call out in case it drew the shooter's attention. Instead she pulled her phone out of her pocket and dialed 911.

Her throat was so tight she could barely speak when the operator answered, her breaths coming in gasps as she relayed the address and what was happening. She told the woman that Easton and Jamie were both armed DEA agents, and that she didn't know how many shooters were out there.

As she spoke, Jamie and Wyatt appeared from behind the far side of the house, and raced over the open ground between the house and the cabin. Mr. C stood on the end of the porch holding a pistol in his left hand, and he wasn't backing down.

A scream built in her throat as more shots ripped through the tense silence, this time coming from a different direction.

Oh my God, they've surrounded us.

Her heart moved back down her throat when Mr. C stepped off the porch, unhurt, and rushed toward the barn as fast as his bad leg would allow. Leaving the shelter and protection of the house to come to their aid.

"They're still shooting at us," she told the operator, her voice tight with fear. A horse snorted in its stall.

"From at least two different directions—west and south."

The woman told her to stay on the line to keep her informed. "Okay," Piper whispered, her gaze glued to Easton. Beyond the open doorway, darkness covered the pastures and the forest. So many good, concealed positions for a shooter to wait.

"Piper, *run*!"

A streak of terror hit her at the desperation in that familiar voice. Seconds later she watched in horror as Greg appeared out of nowhere, racing toward her across the pasture. Before he'd made it halfway, he cried out and fell, the report of a rifle echoing through the darkness.

Oh Christ, they got him. "No!" She took a lurching step toward the open door but Mr. C's gravelly voice stopped her cold.

"Stay put. Easton will get him," he ordered from the front of the barn.

Heart in her throat, she stayed where she was and told the operator to send an ambulance, watching helplessly as Easton raced out into the darkness across the pasture. Greg was crumpled in a ball on the ground, groaning. His weak voice carried to her as he tried to raise a hand and wave Easton off.

"N-no. They're…coming," he wheezed out.

Easton kept running. The crack of a rifle sounded from somewhere behind him in the woods. Piper's heart shot into her throat, her gaze glued to Easton. *They missed. He's okay.*

Easton raced flat out across the pasture and Piper held her breath. A few seconds later he reached Greg, grabbed him under the arms and hauled him up across his shoulders. Greg's scream of agony pierced the night, making tears prick her eyes.

Her heart slammed against her ribs as Easton raced

back toward the barn, using the fence and shrubbery as concealment. More cracks from the rifle echoed in the stillness. He ran past her into the barn and went straight to the closest stall, lying Greg on his back on a pile of straw.

Piper grabbed a flashlight hanging on the wall and rushed after him. She switched it on, aimed it at them and held back a gasp as Easton peeled Greg's bloody hands away from his middle to reveal the bullet hole there. Blood pumped out of the wound, dark and glistening in the beam of light.

She dropped to her knees beside Greg. He forced his eyes open, squinted against the sudden light. "Greg."

He struggled to focus on her, his eyes so full of fear and pain it tore at her insides. "Piper."

"I'm here. I'm right here," she told him, grabbing one of his blood-slick hands and holding it tight. She held the flashlight steady as Easton went to grab a first aid kit from the workbench near the front door.

Greg bared his teeth and let out a horrible cry, then shook his head slightly and grimaced, his deep blue gaze locked on hers. One of the horses stomped its foot and snorted nervously. "R-run," he said, voice urgent as he tried to push her away.

"No, I'm going to help you. Easton and I." She set down the flashlight, aiming it at his belly. Then she stripped off the flannel shirt she wore, leaving her in an undershirt, and wadded it up before pressing it to his wound with both hands. Hard.

He yelled, his entire body jerking against the pain, but there was no escape. "I know it hurts, I'm sorry," she murmured. "I have to keep pressure on it." He was sweating, shaking.

She cupped the side of his scruffy, beaten face. My God, what those animals had done to him. "Greg, you have to lie still. The police are on the way, and an ambulance. They'll be here in just a few minutes, okay? You have to hang on." Seeing him suffering this way was awful.

He shook his head, as if he knew he was dying. "You have…to run. You're not safe here," he wheezed.

"I'm not leaving. We're pinned down."

Easton came back with the kit and leaned over him, his voice as hard as his expression as he dug out some gauze pads and handed them to her. "How many are out there?"

"Th-three." Greg gasped, shuddered. "Gonna…come for her. Leave me. Get her outta here."

"Is Gallant one of them?" Easton demanded.

Greg managed a nod and Piper squeezed his hand tighter, willing him to hang on. God, there was so much blood. The smell of it turned her stomach.

"Was moving…east."

Easton got on his phone and began giving rapid instructions to whoever he'd called.

Greg focused back on her face, and the sheen of tears that flooded his eyes nearly broke her. "S-sorry. Tried to stop this." His lips pressed together, nostrils flaring, and turned his head to the side, a stream of blood trickling out of the corner. He spat it out and gasped, his icy grip clutching her hand. "Gallant's goon saw you carrying something from the shed." He paused, gasped again. "Then he ordered the attack."

The tears she'd been fighting flooded her eyes. He'd known she was in danger, had pushed past the pain in his battered body and summoned the strength to somehow escape Gallant and his men, then take off through the woods in a last-ditch attempt to warn her before they shot him down. He'd let her down so many times in the past, but tonight he'd risked his life to protect her.

"Please go," he rasped out, his strength already fading fast.

"Shhh," she soothed. "Already told you, I'm not leaving. Just be still so I can slow the bleeding." No amount of pressure she applied was going to help him now, he'd lost so much blood, but she hoped he didn't realize it. The bullet had hit an artery. His belly and lap were already soaked in blood and he was deep in shock.

He gazed up at her, eyes filled with torment. "Still love you," he slurred. "Always."

"I know," she murmured, and wiped away tears with her shoulder before focusing back on the blood-soaked gauze she pressed to his wound.

Greg focused on Easton, who had ended his phone call, his attention riveted beyond the barn doorway. "She deserves…better than what I gave her," Greg gasped out. Easton's gaze snapped to his, anger burning there. "Take…take care of her for me."

Easton nodded once. "I will."

The simple conviction in his voice had her biting back a sob. She loved Easton, and even though Greg's past actions had hurt and humiliated her, she didn't want him to die, least of all like this, afraid and in pain. But the blood continued to soak the gauze pads Easton had given her. It didn't seem to matter how hard she pressed, she couldn't slow the bleeding. *Please don't let him die.*

People rushed into the opposite end of the barn. Wyatt, Jamie and Charlie. Then Mr. C's gruff voice split the quiet.

"I'll stay with them," he said to Easton as he shuffled his way over, moving twice as fast as she'd seen him since the stroke. "You and the others go get those sons of bitches."

Fear congealed in her stomach at the thought of Easton and the others trying to hunt down Gallant and his men. Piper opened her mouth to argue but Easton stopped her with a terse shake of his head.

"No," he said tersely. "I have to go. You stay here

with Greg and my dad, where you'll be safe."

A wave of dread crashed over her. She couldn't take it if anything happened to him. "Please just wait, the police are on the way—"

It was a waste of breath. Easton was already pushing to his feet, and the hard mask on his face sent a shiver up her spine. She'd never seen this side of him before, the stone cold operator inside the devil-may-care man she'd known for so long. He was going out there no matter what, and nothing she said or did would change his mind.

Chapter EIGHTEEN

Whoever had come onto his land to hunt his family tonight was going to die.

Rage and adrenaline blasted through Easton as he turned to face the others. “I’m going after Gallant.” His voice was a menacing growl. The cops might be on their way but Easton wasn’t waiting around for them, and he wasn’t allowing the attackers to target his family again.

“I’ll go with you,” Wyatt said.

Easton nodded. “Jamie—”

“I’ll check the western perimeter.”

“I’m coming with you,” Charlie said to him.

Jamie whirled to face her, expression like a thundercloud. “No way.”

“I’m going.” She barely acknowledged him, her voice pure steel. Easton didn’t argue, because Charlie was more than capable of taking care of herself out there, and trusted Jamie to have her back.

“All of you watch your sixes out there,” his dad told

them.

"Be careful," Piper said, her gaze locked on him, eyes full of fear.

She had both hands pressed against Greg's stomach, her skin stained and slick with his blood. In shock and afraid, but hanging in there and doing what needed to be done. He loved her so damn much, and he was going to make sure Gallant didn't get near her.

He nodded once, softened his expression to reassure her. "I will. You stay here with my dad and Austen. Love you." He turned to Wyatt before she could argue, the operator in him needing to move, to end this threat right the fuck now. They'd use their knowledge of the land and track the attackers down. "Let's go."

In the thin beams of moonlight streaming through the open barn door, his brother's face was set in harsh lines. Wyatt was ready to kick some ass. He handed Easton a rifle he'd brought from the house and together they moved to the south entrance. They paused on either side of the doorway.

Outside, everything was quiet, the porch light illuminating the backyard. Not good. The moment they set foot outside the protection of the barn, they'd be exposed. But they couldn't sit here and wait for the shooters to come get them.

Though he hated to leave the others here, he had no choice, and his dad would do everything in his power to keep the two women safe. It had to be enough because Easton and Wyatt had to take Gallant down to eliminate the threat.

In full op mode, he darted out of the barn and ran for the shadows hugging the east side of the barn, dropped to his belly in the grass behind the pasture fence. Wyatt sprawled next to him a few seconds later and together they scanned the area. "He'll be in the woods."

Wyatt nodded. "We'll cut him off."

Easton geared up for the coming run, then shot to his feet and took off down the fence line. He'd grown up hunting with the rifle in his hands, but right now he wished he had his M4 with him, and night optics.

Just as he reached the far end of the pasture, a shot rang out. The top rail beside him exploded into a shower of splinters. He veered right and kept running, aiming for the cover of the trees. He couldn't see anyone but he now had a good idea where the next shooter was.

Behind him, a crash splintered the quiet, followed by a loud whoosh. He ducked and whirled to see the south end of the barn completely engulfed in flames.

Piper!

A figure darted away from the burning building. Gallant. The bastard had somehow doubled back without them noticing and firebombed the barn.

Easton didn't have time to go after him. His only thought was to protect Piper and get the others out of there. The automatic sprinkler system would go on, but that wouldn't stop the smoke and Piper and the others had to get out.

Wyatt's running steps pounded behind him as he ran for the barn, heart in his throat. Gallant had lit one end of the barn to force the occupants out the other end. There had to be a shooter waiting to take them out when they did.

He aimed for the north end of the barn, rifle up, scanning the darkness beyond. It was hard enough to see anything out there, but the flames ruined his ability to see beyond the barn.

He was halfway to it when a flurry of movement erupted from the north end. His lungs seized, a cry of warning building in his throat, then big shadows began flowing out of the open door.

Horses. His dad and Austen must have opened the stalls and flushed the horses out.

The animals raced out into the night, their wet, glistening bodies silhouetted by the glow of the flames on the other end of the barn. Heat licked over his skin as he got closer, the acrid smoke drifting on the breeze thick enough to make his throat burn and his eyes water.

Whinnying and shying in fear, the horses bolted out of the barn and raced around in confusion. Then he saw Austen emerge with his father, his arm draped over her strong shoulders as she hustled him outside, using the cover the confused mass of horses provided, and hunkered down behind the cover of the barn's eastern wall.

No Piper.

"Where's Piper?" he shouted, but Austen was already up and racing back into the burning building. It relieved him a little that she'd been a firefighter, that she was trained for this, but that was still the woman he loved in there and he wouldn't be okay until he knew Piper was all right.

He and Wyatt had almost reached the edge of the pasture when she and Piper emerged moments later, dragging Greg by his armpits. "Stay d—"

The upper railing of the fence exploded to his right.

He ducked and kept running, had no idea where the shot had come from. He reached the barn just as Austen and Piper dragged Greg over to where Easton's dad crouched against the barn wall, pistol in hand.

Easton skidded to his knees beside Piper. He dropped the rifle and took her face in his hands. Those hazel-green eyes focused on him, wide but clear. "Christ," he muttered and crushed her to him.

"I'm okay," she said in a small voice, arms clinging to his back, her words muffled by his chest. He glanced to the left to see Wyatt holding Austen. His dad was kneeling next to Greg.

"He's unconscious," his father said.

Easton nodded and scanned the immediate vicinity. Every second he stayed here cost him the chance of hunting down Gallant, and right now they were all grouped together in one tempting target. He couldn't go after the shooters until Piper and the others were safely behind solid cover, but with Gallant and at least two other shooters on the loose, was anywhere on the property secure anymore?

"We'll go in the house," his dad said. "You boys go. We'll be okay."

Screw that. Easton swiveled and faced the house's back porch. That damn light on was going to get someone killed if they tried to get back inside now.

Seeing no other alternative, he picked up his rifle and aimed it at the porch light. Glass shattered as the bullet hit, plunging the back yard into relative darkness. The flickering flames on the barn were dying out, but there was no time to waste. They'd have to risk moving now. "Let's go."

He grabbed Piper's hand and hauled her to her feet. "You run straight across the backyard and into the kitchen. Don't stop, no matter what happens. Got me?"

"Yes," she answered.

When he turned to look at the others Austen already had his dad on his feet, her arm solid around his waist. Wyatt had Greg draped over his wide shoulders. "I'll cover all of you." He moved toward the burning end of the barn, raised his rifle to his shoulder and aimed into the darkness beyond toward the western pasture. "Go."

They ran. Their rushing steps hustled over the grass and gravel behind him as he fired several closely-spaced shots to keep any would-be shooters pinned down. The back screen door slapped shut. "Wyatt?" he called out, loud as he dared.

"Meet you in the eastern pasture in a minute."

Perfect.

Leaving Piper and the others in the best cover he could offer at the moment, he turned and ran through the darkness toward the eastern pasture. Wyatt burst out of the cellar trap door and ran toward him, weapon up and ready.

The report of a rifle echoed through the night and a round sizzled past his head.

Easton whirled toward the direction the shot had come from, savage satisfaction roaring through him. *You just gave yourself away, asshole.* A fatal mistake.

Rage pumped hot in Easton's veins but he forced it back and kept his gaze trained on the darkened tree line beyond the pasture. The shooter was out there somewhere, and Easton hoped it was Gallant. Because Easton was going to hunt him down.

Up ahead beyond the pasture, the dense band of forest beckoned. He knew every inch of the ground here. Gallant and his men might have the advantage of surprise, concealment and night vision capability, but they didn't know the land like he and Wyatt did. Didn't know the trails and the shortcuts that led to the road, where the shooter was likely heading.

And now that Easton and Wyatt were both coming after him, the bastard would either have to risk attacking them flat out, or run.

He slipped into the woods, carefully placing his steps to make the least amount of noise possible on the carpet of fallen leaves. The sweet, earthy scent wrapped around him, giving him comfort and added strength. He'd been hunting out here since he was a kid, knew every inch of this property.

A gnarled, ancient oak tree that marked the start of a footpath stood sentinel to his right, its huge canopy of spreading branches still adorned with turning leaves. Easton slipped behind the massive trunk and waited, listening, while Wyatt paused behind a broken trunk a few yards away.

Gallant was nothing but a thug who'd run with gangsters and wannabes on the streets. Now he was cut off from his men and up against two SOF trained Marines in the dark, on their home turf. Easton hoped the bastard was the one in front of him right now, and that Gallant was shitting his pants.

Nothing moved in the stillness on the forest floor. The only sound was the breeze blowing through the branches overhead, a gentle sighing with an occasional creak.

Easton paused, pulse beating steady and slow as he waited for his quarry to make a move. The underbrush was too thick for a man to move through without giving himself away and slowing him down. That left the footpath as his only remaining escape route to the road, other than trying to get past Easton and Wyatt.

Either way, he wasn't making it out of here tonight.

A quiet snap sounded behind him and slightly to the left. Easton turned his head a fraction and focused on the spot, waiting in place. A minute later, leaves rustled.

Nice and calm, Easton eased around the huge tree trunk and angled his upper body to get a look. Out of the corner of his eye, he caught movement to his left.

Gotcha.

He stepped out from behind cover and swung the barrel of his rifle toward the noise as he moved forward, knowing Wyatt would be close behind him. It was too dark for him to see his target. He had to rely on only sound and instinct as he followed his prey along the edge of the footpath, tracking him through the darkened forest.

Just as they neared the edge of the road that bordered the eastern side of their property, Easton saw a man's silhouette dart between the trees. He ran forward, caught sight of his target again and fired once.

A sharp cry mixed with the report of the rifle, followed by a dull thud as the man hit the ground.

Rifle to his shoulder, Easton rushed straight for the wounded man, who was sprawled on his side, unmoving. Branches snapped as someone ran off to the right.

Two of them.

Easton spun to take aim at the second man, dropped to one knee as a shot rang out, striking the tree behind him. The road was only forty or fifty feet up the path now.

Moving forward in a crouch, he carefully maneuvered through the brush, using his familiarity with the terrain to angle his way toward the edge of the road, and paused.

Wyatt was to his left, on one knee beside the fallen man. "Dead," he murmured, his quiet voice carrying through the air, and checked the dying man for more weapons. "Not Gallant."

Gallant must be the one trying to get to the road. Easton flexed his fingers around his rifle. *One down, one to go.* On this side of the property, anyway. There was still one more man unaccounted for if Greg's numbers had been correct.

Peering through the last screen of trees between him and the road, Easton spotted a vehicle parked on the shoulder. "He's gonna run for the car," he whispered to Wyatt, who had moved up behind him.

"He won't make it." Raw rage filled his brother's deep voice.

Nope. Trusting his brother to have his back, Easton crept forward, watching the far tree line, keeping the car in his sights. A blur of movement shot out of the trees, and a sliver of light showed Gallant's profile for a split second as he raced by.

Easton aimed through the trees, finger on the trigger, but Gallant managed to dive behind the car for cover before Easton could get a shot off.

He cursed under his breath. "He's at the car." Easton broke from cover and raced toward it, his feet flying over the carpet of branches and fallen leaves. The car engine roared to life and the tires squealed as it took off, spraying up leaves and gravel.

Easton burst through the trees a heartbeat later and fired twice at the rear window. Glass shattered. Wyatt appeared beside him and fired at a rear tire as Easton fired at the back of the front seat. A loud pop followed. The BMW veered and skidded, sliding off the road, and slammed sideways into a tree with a loud crash.

Before the vehicle had even come to rest, Easton and Wyatt were charging toward it. Easton caught movement in the driver's seat. Gallant was struggling to shove the inflated air bag out of his way. Blood glistened on his face and his right arm, where one of Easton's bullet had torn through his shoulder.

You're fucking mine.

Easton ripped open the passenger door, leaving Wyatt to cover him. Gallant grabbed for the weapon on the passenger seat as Easton dove inside and slammed his fist against the side of Gallant's bleeding face.

The guy grunted and fumbled to bring the pistol up but Easton grabbed his wrist and wrenched it down and back. Bone snapped.

Gallant screamed and threw a punch with his other hand but Easton dodged it, grabbed the fucker by the back of the shirt and dragged him across the passenger seat and out of the car.

With a low snarl Easton threw Gallant onto the pavement and rolled him facedown, seizing both his wrists. He held them behind Gallant, pinning him there with his weight.

The son of a bitch was writhing, growling in pain, but Easton didn't give a shit. "How many men did you bring here besides Greg?" he demanded, squeezing the broken wrist.

Gallant howled and arched, trying to throw him off. Easton didn't budge.

"How many, asshole?" he yelled, out of patience. Piper, Austen and his dad were undefended back at the house. This pathetic son of a bitch had tried to kill them all.

"Two," the guy snarled through gritted teeth, a trickle of blood snaking down the side of his face.

If he was telling the truth, it meant the dead guy Easton had just shot, and one more. "Where's the other one?"

The guy was rigid beneath him, low growls of pain escaping his clamped lips. "I don't know."

"Fuck you. *Where*?"

Gallant grunted. "I dunno. West. Maybe southwest."

Probably moving to the road on the west side of the property.

Still straddling Gallant's prone body, Easton kept hold of the bastard's wrists with one hand and pulled out his phone with the other to dial Jamie. His teammate had a Bluetooth in.

Jamie picked up but didn't say anything, alerting Easton that he was either in pursuit or taking cover somewhere.

"There's one shooter left," Easton told him. "Likely moving west, toward the road. Gallant and another of his guys are down and cops should be here soon. Report in when you can."

"Copy," Jamie whispered back.

Easton disconnected and dialed the lead detective. After telling him what was going on and their location, the sound of distant sirens reached him. His next call was to his dad, who picked up immediately. "We got Gallant, and one of the shooters is down. Jamie and

Charlie are in pursuit of the last one. You guys okay there?"

"I can hear the cops coming, they're almost here. But Greg's not gonna make it."

Easton heaved out a sigh. Much as he hated the son of a bitch for what he'd done to Piper, he didn't want her to see her ex die in front of her. She had to have been thoroughly traumatized by what she'd seen and gone through tonight. He knew she was strong enough to deal with it though. "Can you take Piper upstairs—"

"She won't leave him."

Hell. "All right. I'll be there as soon as I can." He ended the call, shifted his grip on Gallant's wrists.

"Fucking let go of my wrist," he snarled, the sirens growing louder.

Easton reined himself in. "You're lucky to still be breathing, asshole. Everyone else you brought here tonight is either dead or about to be."

Blue and red strobe lights reflected off the side of the BMW as the cops turned the corner and raced toward them. Gallant shot Easton a look of pure hatred over his good shoulder. "You're a dead man walking, Colebrook. The whole cartel knows about you. They know where you live. They know where your family and Piper are."

"Shut him the hell up before I do," Wyatt growled behind him.

With pleasure. "Yeah, and they won't touch any of us now that you've fucked up. Know what else? You'll be going back to jail for a damn long time, and the entire cartel will turn their backs on you. Even if you live long enough to get out, you'll already be dead to them."

He shoved upward and stood when the cop cars roared up and stopped yards away. Easton set his rifle on the ground and raised his hands to put the cops at ease.

The closest car's doors popped open and the lead detective jumped out, along with the FBI agents Easton had met before. “You both okay?” the detective called out.

Easton nodded. “We’re good. One shooter’s down in the woods over there,” he said, nodding in the direction of the body. “Greg Rutland is in the house with the others, looks like he won’t make it. My teammate and sister are going after the last shooter.”

The man nodded and strode over to hunker down beside Gallant. “Brandon Gallant, you have the right to remain silent.”

“Fuck you, and save your breath. I know my goddamn rights.”

Easton tuned them out and went with the FBI agents to answer their questions. He glanced over as the detective hauled Gallant to his feet. Blood soaked his face and arm and his grimace of pain filled Easton with satisfaction.

He hoped the bastard was in serious pain for a long time, but more than anything, all Easton wanted was to get back to Piper.

After requesting and receiving permission to go see her, he and Wyatt both raced back to the house. Cops were already on site, searching around the house.

When he hit the backyard the back door opened and Piper flew out of it. Her lap and shirt were stained with Greg’s blood. She raced over the damp grass toward him, the mixture of grief and relief on her face shredding him. Easton caught her as she leapt at him and locked his arms around her, burying his face against her soft hair.

Her arms clung to his shoulders. “He’s dead,” she whispered in a ragged voice that broke his heart. “Was gone before the paramedics got here.”

“I’m so sorry, sweetness.” That had to have been so hard for her to witness.

She nodded and pressed harder to him, her arms holding on so tight her muscles shook. “I’m just so glad you're okay."

"Yeah, I'm okay."

She shuddered, sucked in a shaky breath and held him tighter. "I love you. I love you so much."

Easton squeezed his eyes shut as his heart turned over. He'd wanted to hear those words from her for so damn long. "Love you too." She was his now, and he was never letting her go.

He bent and lifted her into his arms, intending to carry her into the house but Piper stopped him with a hand on his shoulder, her eyes full of worry. "Where are Charlie and Jamie?"

Chapter NINETEEN

Jamie's pulse pumped hard and fast as he ran through the tangle of trees ahead of him. The other shooter was somewhere out front, concealed by the thick forest and its underbrush.

"Psst, over here," Charlie called out in a whisper that carried through the darkness.

He skidded to a stop, turned in time to see her veer off to the left and disappear from view behind a group of trees. Cursing under his breath, he changed direction and raced after her. What the hell was she doing?

It drove him nuts that she was even out here with him right now, placing herself in this kind of danger. She was a computer analyst, not a trained operative, and he'd never forgive himself if anything happened to her out here.

What the hell had her family been thinking, letting—no, *encouraging* her to partner with him for something like this? Once this was all over, he was going to rip into Easton for putting her in such danger.

His heart pumped hard as he ran, concern for her

driving him to run faster, faster. She'd taken a path he hadn't noticed before. He turned up it and charged after her, praying he got between her and the last shooter in time to protect her.

"I see him. He's heading for the road."

Her words floated back to him through the trees, and his gut tightened. "Stay there and don't move," he ordered, slapping branches out of his way with one hand, the rifle Wyatt had given him in the other.

He didn't make it in time.

A second after he caught sight of Charlie up ahead, he spotted the shooter, who was whirling to fire. Before he could shout at her to get down, she raised her own rifle, aimed and fired two shots in rapid succession.

Her target, partially hidden from his view by the trees, grunted and hit the ground with a solid thud. Weapon up and ready, Jamie charged past Charlie and straight for him.

When he cleared the last of the trees in the way, the guy was on his back, groaning, not moving. Blood glistened on his chest, streamed out of his mouth. Shot through the lung.

Jamie kicked the dying man's rifle out of reach and knelt to search him. He found a wallet and a backup weapon. When he placed two fingers beneath the angle of the man's jaw, he wasn't surprised there was no pulse.

"Is he dead?" Charlie asked softly from behind him.

"Yeah." He didn't know if she'd ever seen a dead body before or not, but he was pretty damn sure she'd never shot anyone before. Fuck.

Pushing to his feet, he slid the wallet into the front pocket of his jeans and turned to stand between her and the body so she wouldn't have to see it. She still had the rifle in her hands but it was too dark for him to see her expression. Probably better that way.

"Come on," he said in a low voice, reaching out to

catch her hand. Her fingers were cold and he rubbed his thumb over them to help warm them.

She followed without a word, docile as a lamb. That and her icy hands told him everything he needed to know about her true emotional state. She was in shock, no matter how much she didn't want to admit it.

As he led her back through the woods, he pulled out his cell to call Easton and let him know the last shooter was down, and that he and Charlie were about to emerge from the trees.

"Copy that," Easton said. "Perimeter's secure and the cops are moving to your position now. We'll meet you at the house."

Jamie put his phone back into his pocket and kept moving. The entire property was going to be crawling with cops and Feds in a matter of minutes.

By then he wanted Charlie back safe inside the house with a mug of something hot and a blanket around her shoulders. Her home had just been hit and she'd killed one of the attackers, and he wished like hell none of it had ever happened. They were all in for a long night while they gave statements and answered questions.

A patch of bloody grass glistened at the edge of the west pasture. Jamie changed course and blocked her view as he led her back toward the house, relief that it was over warring with irritation.

The threat might be over now but he was amped up on adrenaline and the sight of Charlie standing there aiming her rifle at the shooter only reminded him of what could have happened to her tonight. He was impressed as hell, but that didn't matter.

She was trouble. He'd known it from the first time they'd met, and it turned out she had a wild, stubborn streak in her just like Easton.

When the house came into view, he could see the cops already fanning out across the yard. He stopped, turned to face her, struggling to sort out his emotions. Her hand was still cold in his. She stirred him up more than any other woman ever had.

He didn't like the way she threatened his control. Didn't *want* to want her, especially since she was Easton's sister but there was no way he could keep his distance right now.

"You okay?" he murmured.

"Fine." The word was soft but curt.

He sighed, fighting the urge to wrap his arms around her. She wasn't okay, but he respected her need to pretend she was. "He would have shot you if you hadn't pulled the trigger." Dammit, he couldn't get that thought out of his head.

She nodded, jaw tight. "I know." A tremor snaked through her, and he couldn't take it anymore.

Without a word he tugged her close and wrapped his arms around her. She was stiff at first, but when all he did was hold her, she relaxed. "Cold?"

"A little."

He stood there for a few minutes, running his hands up and down her back, keeping her tight to his chest to warm her. Her sweet scent teased him, her firm curves molding to his body in a way that made him bite back a growl.

He squeezed her and pressed a kiss to the top of her head. "Better?"

A nod.

Lowering his arms, he eased back a few inches to stare down at her in the wash of light coming through the back windows of the main house. "You're trouble," he said.

And yet he couldn't stay away from her. The urge to protect her was overwhelming and he couldn't shut it off.

Her gaze flicked up to meet his, those deep, dark eyes

focusing on him with a spark of anger. "They attacked my home, my family. Was I just supposed to sit on my ass and wring my hands while you guys handled it alone?"

Yes. He didn't dare say it aloud, because he suspected she'd rip his balls off if he did. "No, but I didn't expect you to run for the nearest rifle and chase after the shooter, either."

"I was backing you up."

"No, you took off on your own and put yourself in danger. That's not how teammates back each other up."

And I couldn't get to you in time.

That's really what was bothering him. The thought that she could have been hurt or killed tonight.

Her eyes widened in outrage. "Just because I'm a woman doesn't mean I'm weak or defenseless. You think that just because of my gender and occupation, I don't know how to handle a weapon? I was raised in a household of four Marines, and even if I didn't serve like they did, I still shoot like a Marine."

He struggled not to smile at her sass and the pride in her voice. The way she'd faced that shooter and taken him down had both shocked and impressed the hell out of him, and he didn't do either of those things easily. "Yeah, you sure as hell do." God, he wanted to kiss her.

She blinked and eyed him in suspicion. "That's right."

Kissing her now would be a really stupid move, but it was hard not to. Charlie burned with an irrepressible energy that was palpable the moment she walked into a room. She did something to him, brought the most possessive and protective parts of him raging to the surface, and tonight had made that even stronger.

"Remind me never to piss you off."

She glared up at him. "Too late."

He smothered a laugh, fighting the urge to crush her

to him and pillage that sassy mouth. Her eyes glittered up at him in the dimness with pure annoyance, and he lost the battle.

To hell with it.

Unable to help himself, he cupped the back of her head with one hand and leaned in to capture her mouth with his. She sucked in a swift breath, put her free hand on his chest as if to push away.

No way. Not after the way she'd scared him to death and then taken that shooter out. Not with this need to protect her burning inside him.

He wrapped his free arm around her waist and hauled her up against him, groaned at the feel of her softness melded to his body. It was the first time he'd allowed himself to be the aggressor with her.

That night at the club, he'd simply followed her cues and given her a taste of what she'd wanted. The memory had haunted him ever since. The idea of any other man putting his hands on her made him insane and it drove him nuts because she'd made it abundantly clear she didn't want anything serious.

Well, he was as serious about her as he'd ever been about anything, way more than he'd been with any other woman. Now, he was the one in control and this was more than a kiss—he was staking a claim. Part of him didn't care that he was making out with her on the lawn within sight of the house where any member of her family might see them.

The feel and taste of her, those little sounds of pleasure she made at the back of her throat as he tangled his tongue with hers made him want to drag her back into the woods for privacy and fuck her deep and hard. It took monumental effort for him to ignore the impulse and settle for this hard, hungry kiss.

Instinct told him that to win Charlie, he had to leave her wanting more. Even if it killed him to pull away, she needed to know she didn't call the shots between them.

More sirens sounded to the west, where they'd just come from, giving him the perfect excuse to end the kiss. He raised his head to stare down at her in the dimness, fierce satisfaction raging through him at the almost drugged look in her dark eyes. Her lips were shiny and swollen and her hair was mussed.

"Cavalry's finally here," he murmured, rubbing his thumb over her satiny cheek.

Her eyes cleared and she licked her lips, a slow smile playing at the edges of her mouth. "Late as usual."

"Mmm," he agreed, and just because he couldn't help himself, he went back for one more taste. This time slower, tender. Savoring her because he didn't know when he'd get to taste her again. "Let's get back to the house before they send out a search party for us."

Blue and red flashing lights came up the driveway, another convoy of police cars roaring toward the house. The moment Charlie walked into the house, both her brothers and father were there to pull her into a tight hug, then Austen and Piper hugged her as well.

It did his heart good to see how much they all loved her. His own family was back in southern California and he didn't get to see them that often. He was sure as hell calling them tonight.

As expected, the Feds took the lead in the investigation, splitting everyone up to get their individual stories while officers and agents combed the property. By the time they were done with him, it was two in the morning and he still had to drive back to Alexandria before he could get some sleep.

Charlie was talking with her dad and her brothers on the couch in front of the fireplace, her head resting on her father's shoulder. The sight made Jamie's heart squeeze.

He was on his way to the front door with his duffel

when Charlie came out of the dining room. "You leaving?" she asked.

He turned to face her. "Yeah."

Her eyebrows pulled together in a frown. "So you were just going to leave without saying goodbye?"

"You were busy with your family and I didn't want to take you away from them."

She searched his eyes. "Were you going to call me at least?"

"Yeah, I was. I need to go now, though." Nothing more was going to happen between them, at least not tonight and not here, in her father's house.

But he knew this was far from over between them and it was only a matter of time until she wound up underneath him. If they took things farther after this…

"Wait," she exclaimed, and rushed over to him. He stopped, tensed as she drew near, those dark eyes locked with his. She stood a foot away from him, her sugary-sweet scent wrapping around him. "When will I see you again?"

"Depends."

She raised an eyebrow. "On?"

"On what you're willing to give. Because if you want to see me again, there's something you should know."

Her eyes gleamed with interest and she folded her arms across her chest, deliberately bringing his gaze to her luscious breasts. His lips quirked. "And what's that?" she asked, the hint of a taunt in her voice.

He stared into her eyes as he answered, convinced he'd read her right. She wanted a challenge. Well, he was that and more. "I play for keeps." Leaning down, he brushed his lips across her cheek. "See you later, Trouble," he murmured. "Say goodbye to your family for me." Then he picked up his bag and walked out into the cold night air.

****

Pinned and helpless beneath the hot, hard male body on top of her in the darkness, Piper had never felt so free. Or more alive.

The last few hours had passed in a complete blur of questioning and interviews by both the police and FBI. Then the medical examiner had come to take Greg's body to the morgue.

Easton had pulled her into his lap on the easy chair next to the fire and cuddled her while everyone filed out of the house at last. Charlie and Mr. C had both stopped to rub her back and offer their condolences before heading upstairs. In the quiet that followed, she'd finally allowed the tears she'd been holding back to fall.

It didn't matter that she'd already grieved for Greg once before, after their marriage had ended and she'd walked out. She'd never imagined being there at the end to hold his hand and watch him die right in front of her while she sat next to him, helpless.

Thankfully Easton had seemed to understand. He'd sat with her like that until the logs in the grate burned down to glowing embers, then smoothed the hair back from her face and kissed her gently. She'd cupped his bearded cheek and kissed him with all the love and need in her heart, desperate to feel the magic of their connection, to chase away the sadness and the horror with the tenderness and joy that could only come from making love with him.

I want inside you, he'd whispered, then picked her up and carried her into the cabin, straight to this bed, where he'd laid her down and undressed her in the darkness.

Now there was nothing but the feel of him anchoring her to the bed, the slam of her heart against her ribs and the rush of her uneven breaths in her ears as she waited for him to push inside her and soothe the empty ache he'd created.

Easton's hand firmed on her hip, holding her in place while the other wound in her hair. She trembled at the intensity of the moment, the intimate quiet surrounding them magnifying the electric anticipation. Even with her eyes closed she could feel the way he watched her, all his focus and control centered on her and her pleasure.

"Ah!" She gasped and arched beneath him as he buried himself deep inside her with one slow thrust, trapping a throttled cry in her throat. Shuddering in his arms, she forced her eyes open to look up at him through the haze of sensation.

Weak light heralding the approaching dawn streamed through the edges of the blinds in the cabin's bedroom, giving just enough illumination for her to see his face as he loomed above her, his weight now propped up on his elbows. Rain pattered on the roof in a soothing rhythm overhead, adding to the cozy, intimate atmosphere.

A whimper tore from her lips as he watched her face. He was so thick and hard inside her, the angle of his thrust so perfect, her aching clit pressed against his pelvis. She spread her thighs wider apart, desperate for more.

The strong hand on her hip squeezed tight, stilling her. "Don't move," he whispered, his mouth inches from her lips as he stared down at her.

She closed her eyes and shuddered. It was too intimate, felt too good. She was so close already, just another few strokes and she'd come. "I…have to," she cried, her entire body tensing. The muscles in her thighs and belly trembled, the pleasure swelling inside her. Unbearable.

"Don't," he said, his quiet voice barely carrying. "Just stay still and look at me."

Somehow she forced her heavy eyelids open and met his heated gaze. He was so thick and hot inside her, filling her completely, each ripple of her internal muscles around his cock sending streamers of fire along her nerve endings.

Holding his gaze for those breathless heartbeats, she felt her heart crack wide open. Her core clenched around him, desperate for him to ease the ache. She cried out as the sensation swelled, her eyes slamming shut, her hands digging into his back and hip, fighting to pump her hips and get the friction she craved.

Easton let out a rough groan, eased back, then surged forward, giving her exactly what she needed. His mouth covered hers in a hot, voracious kiss that stole what little breath she had left. He swallowed her sobs of pleasure as the world dissolved around her, his strength and weight the only things anchoring her as she tumbled into the abyss.

"Ah, God, Piper…" he moaned, then thrust deep and stiffened, his entire body shuddering as his release hit him. She clutched him to her like a woman clinging to the debris of a shipwreck.

In the aftermath, lying there trembling in his arms and her heartbeat galloping in her ears, she held him as close as she could. "I love you," she whispered, her throat and chest clogged with emotion. There was no way she could leave him. But she also didn't know where they went from here. "I love you and I need you."

Easton lifted his head to gaze down at her, his expression so full of torment it made her chest ache. "Then don't go to Minnesota. Come to Alexandria and move in with me instead."

Letting out a deep breath, she gave him a tremulous smile and nodded. "Okay."

His face went blank with surprise for a second, then a huge smile spread across his face. "You will?"

She traced a finger down the side of his scruffy cheek. "Yes. I can't leave. I don't want to lose you and

I'm not leaving you over a job." Even if it was her dream job, he still mattered a thousand times more. "Wherever you are is my home." She had no idea what the future held for them, but she couldn't give up this chance.

He groaned in relief and rested his forehead against hers. "You're not gonna lose me, sweetness. Not ever." Still joined with her, he shifted, propping himself up on one forearm to brush her hair back from her face with his free hand. "You still worried about my job?"

"A little," she admitted. Seeing him in action tonight had been eye-opening, even if she was well aware of what he did for a living.

He sighed and ran his fingers through her hair. "I know what I do is dangerous. But whatever happens, you have to know I'll do whatever it takes to come home to you. All the guys on my team are like Jamie. Dedicated, solid, dependable guys. We look out for each other, always. The most important thing for all of us is to make sure everyone comes home at the end of a mission or deployment."

She nodded and managed a smile, even though she was still scared of what could happen to him. "It's just…you're everything to me," she whispered, swallowing. She'd already lost so much, she couldn't bear it if something happened to him.

Tenderness and understanding filled his eyes. "That goes both ways, sweetness. I know it won't be easy and that I'll be gone a lot and I won't always be able to tell you where I am or where I've been, but you own me, body and soul. And you're already part of my family. They'll be here for you when I can't be, so you won't ever be alone. Not really."

"I like the sound of that," she murmured, filled with so much love she ached with it. Lifting her head to press a kiss to his lips, she wrapped her arms around his back and pulled him down into her embrace, holding him close as they drifted back to sleep.

Epilogue

Three months later

"You having a good Christmas so far?"

Piper smiled at Easton's murmur against the top of her head, his arms around her as they stood by the entryway into the dining room and faced the beautifully set farmhouse table just waiting for the family to gather around it. The air smelled of roasted turkey and the sharp tang of evergreen boughs that decorated the house. "Best one ever." As a child, Christmas had always been her favorite time of year.

"Good. Now go sit while we take it from here." He released her and went to help his brothers carry the platters of food in from the kitchen.

Piper took her usual place along the far side of the table, and the sight of the beautifully laid out decorations and place settings before her set off a bittersweet pang in her chest. After her mother had left them, Piper and her father had made their own traditions together.

Christmas Eves had been spent in the kitchen, making treats to eat together while watching a holiday movie with the fireplace on. After moving here for her senior year of high school, they'd started coming to the Colebrooks' place for carols and hot cider with cinnamon candies melted into it. Everyone sat in front of the fire beside the big, fresh Christmas tree twinkling in the corner of the family room, eating and drinking. Sometimes they played board games, and a few times when it had snowed the boys had hitched up an old sleigh and taken them all on a ride across the pastures.

"Okay, everyone to the table so we can eat this feast," Mr. C called out, shuffling his way in from his study.

A warm glow filled her at the sight of him, the proud patriarch of this family. She loved that gruff old man to death.

After her dad died, Mr. C had continued to invite her over to spend Christmas with the family. She'd come over Christmas Eve and stay the night, and there were always a few gifts under the tree for her when the family gathered around it the next morning. They ate Christmas Day dinner early, at three o'clock, because that's the way Mrs. C had always done it when she was alive, and Piper loved that they were carrying on that tradition.

"Shall we say grace?" Mr. C said when everyone was seated.

Seated next to Easton, Piper looked around the table at everyone. Brody and Trinity were at the far end. Wyatt and Austen opposite her. Charlie to her right and Mr. C at his customary place at the head of the long farmhouse table. Her family.

It might be December ninth instead of the twenty-fifth, but the date itself didn't matter, and this was the only way they could accommodate everyone's schedule. They were together, and time with family was what Christmas was all about.

Piper took Charlie's left hand, then grasped Easton's right. She loved having him here for this, it wouldn't have been the same without him.

He'd been gone a lot these past few months, leaving her to settle into his place in Alexandria mostly alone. He was leaving for another stint in Afghanistan next week and she didn't even want to think about how much she was going to miss him over the next four months. Every moment with him was precious, and she savored them all.

Giving him a little smile, she bowed her head and spotted Grits lying beneath the table at Wyatt's feet, Sarge sprawled on his side a few feet away. Both were awake and alert, ready to gobble up anything that fell from the table.

Piper closed her eyes. They said a short prayer, then toasted both Mrs. C and Piper's dad. Every year the same, and it touched her deeply that they still included her that way.

"They're always in our hearts, and their love is always with us," Mr. C finished, raising his glass in a toast.

"Amen," everyone responded, then took a sip of their drink and began the feast.

The table and sideboard were overflowing with platters and bowls of food. Everyone had pitched in with the prep, and then left the cooking to her and Austen. The best part was, that meant the guys, Charlie and Trinity were on cleanup duty, so after she'd stuffed herself silly, Piper could go lounge on the couch in the family room with Austen and put her feet up.

She loaded her plate with roasted turkey and homemade cranberry sauce, Mrs. C's cream cheese mashed potatoes, stuffing, veggies and gravy. She had seconds of the turkey and potatoes, laughed at Easton, who helped himself to thirds before leaning back and groaning in pleasure/pain.

Free to relax while everyone handled the dishes, she sprawled on the buttery leather sofa opposite the fireplace in the family room and sipped at a mug of apple cinnamon cider while she chatted with Austen. She and Wyatt had officially finished up the renovations on their Victorian house a month ago and were all moved in. They'd invited everyone over last night for a big dinner starring Austen's mama's famous mac 'n cheese, and Piper had brought lemon squares for dessert.

"Hey, and guess what? Wyatt's finally decided to start a therapy dog program for vets, using rescue dogs, and possibly a riding program here too," Austen said.

"That's so great! He'll be amazing at it."

She pushed a dark spiral of hair away from her face. "It'll keep him out of my hair, and out of trouble. How are things in Alexandria, by the way?"

"Good. I've got a teaching job lined up for early January."

Austen's face brightened. "That's great!"

"Yeah, and it'll keep me busy while Easton's overseas. I'm super excited about it. By the time he gets back, I'll only have a month or so left of the school year."

Austen's smile disappeared. "When's he leave again?"

Way too soon. "Next week." She hated him going over there again, but his job meant so much to him and he'd already promised her he wouldn't do it forever. She loved him and wanted him to be happy, so she had to suck it up and be brave.

"You gonna be okay?"

"I'll just take it one day at a time. At least with living in Alexandria I've got Charlie nearby, and I've been spending a little time with Trinity lately too."

Austen's eyes twinkled silver in the firelight. "She's

so freaking awesome."

"I know," she said excitedly, sitting up and tucking her feet beneath her. "She's like a female James Bond."

"Am not."

They turned their heads as Trinity strode toward them from the kitchen, glass of red wine in hand, the deep ruby merlot matching the color of the sweater that hugged her pinup body to perfection.

"I'm retired," Trinity went on, taking the armchair in the corner of the room and draping her legs over one overstuffed arm. "But when I *was* in that line of work, I was much more discreet than 007 ever was." Her red lips curved in a sexy, mysterious smile that had Piper grinning.

"I told her she needs to write a book. And then make it into a screenplay," Charlie said, entering the room with a highball in one hand and one of Piper's pumpkin cheesecake squares in the other. "Would blow the Bond franchise right out of the water."

"Ah, the things I could put on the page," Trinity said with a secret smile.

Piper sipped at her cider as the female conversation flowed around her, comfortable with these women who had become her family as well. Her heart was as full as her belly, and she'd never felt more content. The only thing that dampened her happiness was knowing Easton was going back into harm's way for the next four months.

After the guys cleaned up the dishes, everyone gathered around the fire to visit. Piper curled up in Easton's lap, her head on his solid shoulder, the heat of the fire and the love of the people in the room surrounding her like a warm hug.

"Ready to go to the cabin yet?" he murmured next to her ear.

Longing stirred deep in her belly. She was more than

ready for some alone time with him. Their life together was everything she'd ever hoped for and more.

He'd stood next to her at Greg's funeral with a solid arm around her and a sturdy shoulder for her to cry on. He'd helped her pack up and moved her into his place in Alexandria after her house sold, then put out calls to all his contacts to help find her a dream teaching job that started in the New Year.

"If you are," she answered.

"Did I mention that your big present is there waiting to be unwrapped?"

She sat up immediately. "It is? Why didn't you say so?"

They said goodnight to the others and headed outside into the cold night air. Easton slid an arm around her waist, his hold possessive as they made the short walk over to the cabin. It was dark inside, the air smelling of the fir tree they'd bought yesterday to decorate.

"Stay here for a bit and close your eyes," he told her when he shut the front door behind them, locking out the cold and the rest of the world.

Piper smiled to herself and did as she was told. This had already been the most magical Christmas she'd ever had. She couldn't imagine anything topping it.

"Okay, come in," he called a few minutes later.

She stepped through the living room doorway and a delighted smile broke over her face. He'd turned on the lights on the decorated tree in the corner, and lit a fire in the grate. Flames crackled and popped, throwing a warm orange-yellow glow throughout the room.

When she moved closer, she saw the rest of what he'd done and her heart turned over. A thick quilt was laid out on the old, wide floorboards in front of the hearth, and topped with fluffy pillows for them to lounge on. He'd put a bottle of white wine in a bucket of ice to chill, and there was a plate of little bite-sized chocolate treats next to it.

"Brownies?" she asked.

"Your recipe. I made them myself last night in the house after you went to bed, so I could surprise you."

He was so sweet. "And you saved this many? Now I'm even more impressed."

"Ha ha. Stop mocking me and come down here," he said, holding out a hand.

She curled her fingers around his and let him draw her down to sit beside him on the quilt. With a little grin of anticipation on his lips he picked up a bite of brownie and brought it to her mouth. She took it from his fingers, the rich, decadent flavor bursting on her tongue. *Mmmmm.* "I don't even know how I have room for that, but oh my God, so good," she said.

He hummed in agreement and helped himself to one, then hooked an arm around her waist from behind and dragged her into his lap. She could feel his erection pressing against her bottom, and the thought of making love with him here in front of the fire had her blood heating.

To her, the setting was unbelievably romantic, and that he'd gone to such trouble touched her. She'd never known love could feel this way—all-consuming and yet painful at the same time. Easton owned every bit of her heart. If anything happened to him, she didn't know if she'd survive it.

The thought made her chest constrict. She curled into him, turned to wrap both arms around his shoulders and hold on tight, burying her face in his neck so she could breathe him in.

"Hey," he said, running a hand up and down her back, his strong arms surrounding her. "What's wrong?"

"I love you so much it hurts."

He pulled her away from him and shifted to roll her onto her back, coming down on top of her a moment later. His grin was sexy yet devilish as he stared down at her. “Love you the same way, sweetness.”

She melted under him as he kissed her long and slow, relishing the feel of his hard, heavy body atop hers. Just as her insides began to hum with need, he stopped and rolled off her.

“You can’t offer me my present like that and then just take it away,” she protested.

A low chuckle rumbled from the depths of his chest. “That was part two of your present. Part one is waiting over here,” he said, grasping her hands and pulling her into a sitting position before pointing at the tree.

It was then she noticed the end of a red satin ribbon lying on the floor. He picked it up and handed it to her, and she realized it was woven through the branches. “Time to unwrap your first present,” he said, leaning in to kiss her once more. “You can unwrap me afterward.”

Her lips quirked and she began unwinding the length of ribbon through the branches. He’d really gone to town with it, twining it around every single branch in a complex tangle that quickly began to annoy her until she saw something sparkling deep within the branches next to the trunk.

Her breath caught and she stuck her head into the tree to get a better look, heart pounding. “Oh my God, Easton…” Her throat closed up as she reached out a trembling hand for the diamond ring tied there. She tugged on the little bow to untie it, then pulled out of the tree to face him.

He was on one knee in front of her, a tender smile on his lips. He took the ring from her and gathered her left hand in his, his velvet-brown eyes gazing up at her with complete love and devotion. “Will you marry me, Piper?”

A strangled sound came out of her, half laugh, half sob. She went to her knees in front of him, threw her arms around his neck and squeezed tight. “Yes. Yes, of course I’ll marry you. I would *love* to marry you.”

He chuckled deep in his chest, hugging her in return, then eased her back to slide the ring on her finger. Her cheeks were wet but she didn’t know when she’d started crying. He wiped the tears away, gave her an adoring smile. “Know what this means?”

She looked up from the sparkling diamond and into his eyes. “That I’m finally going to be an actual Colebrook, officially?”

“Well yeah, that too.” His eyes heated, the possessive light there making her heart flutter. “More importantly, it means you’re going to be mine forever. And that I’m going to love you for the rest of my life.”

“You have no idea how much that works for me.” She reached for the top button of his shirt. “Time to unwrap my best present now,” she whispered, and leaned in to kiss that sexy, smiling mouth.

—The End—

Thank you for reading EASTON'S CLAIM. I really hope you enjoyed it and that you'll consider leaving a review at one of your favorite online retailers. It's a great way to help other readers discover new books.

If you liked EASTON'S CLAIM and would like to read more, turn the page for a list of my other books. And if you don't want to miss any future releases, please join my newsletter:

http://kayleacross.com/v2/newsletter/

Complete Booklist

ROMANTIC SUSPENSE

Colebrook Siblings Trilogy

Brody's Vow
Wyatt's Stand
Easton's Claim

Hostage Rescue Team Series

Marked
Targeted
Hunted
Disavowed
Avenged
Exposed
Seized
Wanted
Betrayed
Reclaimed

Titanium Security Series

Ignited
Singed
Burned
Extinguished
Rekindled

Bagram Special Ops Series

Deadly Descent
Tactical Strike
Lethal Pursuit
Danger Close
Collateral Damage

Suspense Series
Out of Her League
Cover of Darkness
No Turning Back
Relentless
Absolution

PARANORMAL ROMANCE
Empowered Series
Darkest Caress

HISTORICAL ROMANCE
The Vacant Chair

EROTIC ROMANCE (writing as ***Callie Croix***)
Deacon's Touch
Dillon's Claim
No Holds Barred
Touch Me
Let Me In
Covert Seduction

Acknowledgements

A shout out to all my wonderful readers, for supporting this new series.

And as always, a huge thanks to my editing team, cover artist, formatter and DH, for all their help in whipping this baby into shape. It takes a village!

About the Author

NY Times and USA Today Bestselling author Kaylea Cross writes edge-of-your-seat military romantic suspense. Her work has won many awards and has been nominated for both the Daphne du Maurier and the National Readers' Choice Awards. A Registered Massage Therapist by trade, Kaylea is also an avid gardener, artist, Civil War buff, Special Ops aficionado, belly dance enthusiast and former nationally-carded softball pitcher. She lives in Vancouver, BC with her husband and family.

You can visit Kaylea at www.kayleacross.com. If you would like to be notified of future releases, please join her newsletter:

http://kayleacross.com/v2/newsletter/

CPSIA information can be obtained
at www.ICGtesting.com
Printed in the USA
FSOW02n1909250916
25394FS